A Hell of a Way To Travel . . .

Clint had less than a second to keep his head from being blown completely off his shoulders. He used that time to grab on to the rail that ran along the top of the stage and swing himself over the edge. His fingers locked around the rail with every ounce of strength he could muster. When his arms reached their limit, his entire body slapped against the side of the stage with an impact he felt all the way down to his toes. Clint's shoulders screamed for mercy, but he some-how managed to hang on as the shotgun blast tore a chunk from the section of roof where he'd just been.

Clint dangled from the stage like a flag at half-mast. His fingers burned, but he couldn't tell if they'd been hit by some buckshot or if they were simply about to snap from the pressure of keeping the rest of him off the ground. It didn't really matter either way. Between the sweat from his hands and blood possibly added to the mix, Clint wasn't going to stay on the coach for long. Every jostling bump that rattled the stage caused him to slip a little farther . . .

THE GUNSMITH

337

PARIAH

J. R. ROBERTS

JOVE BOOKS, NEW YORK

THE BERKLEY PUBLISHING GROUP
Published by the Penguin Group
Penguin Group (USA) Inc.
375 Hudson Street, New York, New York 10014, USA

Penguin Group (Canada), 90 Eglinton Avenue East, Suite 700, Toronto, Ontario M4P 2Y3, Canada
(a division of Pearson Penguin Canada Inc.)
Penguin Books Ltd., 80 Strand, London WC2R 0RL, England
Penguin Group Ireland, 25 St. Stephen's Green, Dublin 2, Ireland (a division of Penguin Books Ltd.)
Penguin Group (Australia), 250 Camberwell Road, Camberwell, Victoria 3124, Australia
(a division of Pearson Australia Group Pty. Ltd.)
Penguin Books India Pvt. Ltd., 11 Community Centre, Panchsheel Park, New Delhi—110 017, India
Penguin Group (NZ), 67 Apollo Drive, Rosedale, North Shore 0632, New Zealand
(a division of Pearson New Zealand Ltd.)
Penguin Books (South Africa) (Pty.) Ltd., 24 Sturdee Avenue, Rosebank, Johannesburg 2196,
South Africa

Penguin Books Ltd., Registered Offices: 80 Strand, London WC2R 0RL, England

PARIAH

A Jove Book / published by arrangement with the author

PRINTING HISTORY
Jove edition / January 2010

ISBN: 978-0-515-14743-8

JOVE®
Jove Books are published by The Berkley Publishing Group,
a division of Penguin Group (USA) Inc.,
375 Hudson Street, New York, New York 10014.
JOVE® is a registered trademark of Penguin Group (USA) Inc.
The "J" design is a trademark of Penguin Group (USA) Inc.

PRINTED IN THE UNITED STATES OF AMERICA

10 9 8 7 6 5 4 3 2 1

ONE

Clint Adams was always amazed by how far a little kindness could stretch. He'd been riding through the Arizona Territories, Tombstone being no more than a day behind him, when he'd stopped in a little town to get a bite to eat. Since he hadn't planned on staying for more than an hour or so, he hadn't even bothered to learn the name of the town. It had a restaurant for him and a trough of water for Eclipse, which were the only two things he was after.

The restaurant was a small establishment run by a family that must have been used to some pretty horrific food because the owner's wife didn't seem to know her way around the kitchen. Clint gnawed on his tough cut of steak, washed it down with some bitter coffee, and was about to pay the damages when he heard a commotion outside in the street.

"What was that?" the middle-aged man asked while his hands were still full of Clint's dirty dishes.

Clint stood up and took some money from his pocket. "I don't know, but it sounded like someone shouting. Maybe I should have a look."

"Aww, you don't have to do that. We got some law

around here and I was just about to offer you some pie that the wife whipped up earlier this afternoon."

So that explained the acrid scent of burnt sugar and blackened dough.

"No," Clint said while doing his best to keep the mix of panic and disgust from showing on his face. "I should definitely go have a look. Someone may be in trouble."

"Are you a lawman?"

Desperate for an excuse to get out of there before the commotion resolved itself and he was forced to sample some poorly made dessert, Clint said, "Yeah. You might say that. This should settle up my bill," he added while tossing some money onto the table. "Keep the rest."

That brightened the owner's face well enough. "Much obliged. I can put it toward the purchase of some spices being brought in by a man who has 'em exported all the way from England."

Or he could pay to hire a real cook. Rather than make that particular suggestion, Clint tipped his hat and hurried out the door. As luck would have it, he wouldn't even need to avoid walking past the restaurant's front window. The shouting was still going on and it was coming from a pair of children being escorted across the street by a tall blonde woman. Clint might have stretched the truth about being a lawman, but he wasn't about to let a lady and two young ones keep screaming until official help arrived.

The blonde woman wore a simple brown dress that was tattered along the hemline and covered in dust. She had a child grasping each of her hands, one of whom was a boy who looked to be around the age of nine, and the other a girl who appeared at least four years younger. The boy had dark skin and short hair, while the girl had the complexion and facial features that hinted at Chinese or some other kind of Asian heritage.

A man in his fifties tugged at the blonde woman's skirts while two more watched and laughed from a few feet away.

All three of the men were covered in enough filth to make it seem as if they'd been dragged from the back of a wagon, and Clint doubted they could pool their resources to form one full set of teeth between them.

"Tell that little bitch to stop screamin' or I'll put my foot in her mouth!" the man tugging the blonde's skirt said.

The blonde swatted at the man's hand and did her best to keep the children away from him. "Don't call her that!" she snapped.

"Then what should I call her? Somethin' tells me we'll be seein' a whole lot of each other."

The other two men chuckled at that, but they didn't take their eyes off the blonde. She was a handsome woman and was unable to hide that fact no matter how high she buttoned her collar or how many shawls she wrapped around her shoulders. Since it wasn't nearly cool enough to warrant so many layers, it seemed she'd been doing her best to avoid this very situation.

After she'd transferred the boy's hand to the same one holding the girl's, the blonde turned so her body was between the men and the children. Without an ounce of fear in her eyes, she turned toward the men and declared, "You won't be seeing us at all!"

"Is that a fact, now?"

"It is. You'll go your way and we'll go ours."

Hooking his thumbs in his gun belt, the man asked, "And what if my way just happens to lead under them pretty skirts of yers?"

"That'll be enough of that," Clint said as he walked up to stand between the woman and all three men.

The blonde looked toward him with relief, but then gathered the children closer and eased away. "Thank you, but we'll be just fine. The sheriff will be along shortly."

"I'm sure he will, ma'am," Clint said. "Why don't you just go along and get him or do whatever it is you need to do. I'll stay and have a word with these three."

The blonde backed away, but was hesitant to do so. Once she made it down the boardwalk a little farther, she sat the children down on a low bench and knelt so she was at their eye level when talking to them.

"Move along, asshole," the first dirty-faced man snarled.

Clint looked at that man and then at the other two. "What's the matter? Can only one of you talk at a time?"

"What if I told you I was her husband and this ain't none of your concern?" the first man asked. The other two remained silent, but they took up a position on either side of him while glaring at Clint.

One quick glance over his shoulder was enough for Clint to see the look on the blonde woman's face. "Seems like the lady is about to hack up her breakfast just from hearing that claim. Makes me think it's not true."

"It don't matter what you think. Step aside and let us pass."

"I'm not wide enough to take up this whole street," Clint said. "If you want to pass, you can surely get around me." Waiting until the men took their first steps in his direction, Clint added, "You might want to give the lady and those children a wide berth."

The three men stopped. Two of them looked at the spokesman for the group, prompting that one to ask, "Or what?"

Shifting his gaze into a cold, hateful stare, Clint replied, "Take another step toward her and find out for yourselves."

The spokesman thought it over for all of two seconds before backing up. When he bumped into his two companions, he straightened his posture and faced Clint much like a rat that just realized it had been forced into a corner. Putting on an unconvincing scowl, he strode toward the blonde.

Clint stepped to one side and placed his hand flat against the man's chest to stop him in his tracks. "Is this man your husband, ma'am?" he called out.

"I don't have a husband," she replied.

Clint smirked and cracked his knuckles. "Well then," he said to the spokesman. "Seems like a bit of bad luck for you."

TWO

The first man to charge at Clint did so without warning. In fact, he seemed to take the spokesman by surprise as well when he rushed forward with his fist swinging at Clint's jaw. Although he was a little surprised by the timing, Clint wasn't shocked to see that one make a run at him before the others. While the other two had been posturing and talking tough, his attacker had been tensing like a bowstring being drawn taut.

Fortunately, the first one to charge also had the most ground to cover. By the time he got close enough to reach Clint, he no longer had a target for his punch. Clint had stepped aside into a wide stance, leaving one foot planted where it was and sliding his other out a few feet. When he felt the man's boot snag against his leg, Clint snapped a quick jab across his face and then pushed him over. The man stumbled and dropped as if he'd accidentally found a half-buried log while charging through a mess of bushes.

The spokesman stayed put while his second companion rushed forward to try his luck with Clint. He was met by a stiff, straight punch to his gut that doubled him over and drove all the wind from his lungs. While he was bent over like that, he left his chin wide open for a straight, upward knee. Clint was more than happy to oblige and used his knee to send the second man staggering away to trip over the first.

"Mister," the spokesman said, "you just called down a whole mess of trouble."

Clint let the man talk, simply because it gave him a few seconds to step away from the other two and square his shoulders with the last upright man.

The spokesman wore a pistol strapped around his waist, but moved slower than molasses in winter when he tried to skin it. Before that man's fingers closed around the grip of his revolver, Clint had already cleared leather and was pointing his modified Colt at him.

"You sure you want to take it this far?" Clint asked. "You and your men can still walk away."

The spokesman gritted his teeth and glared at Clint, but there was no real conviction in his eyes. He was defeated and he knew it. All that remained was for him to hide his fear, and he wasn't doing a very good job of it. Finally, he sputtered, "We'll go . . . but just because we wanna go."

"Of course," Clint replied.

Shifting his eyes to the blonde, the spokesman added, "And when we feel like comin' back, we'll—"

"Think real hard before you finish that sentence," Clint warned.

The spokesman froze with his mouth hanging open. If the words had been physical things, they might have dribbled from the corner of his lip and spilled onto the front of his shirt. Slowly, he turned away from Clint and walked past his two companions. "Come on," he grumbled. "You gonna lay in the street all damn day?"

While the spokesman kept from walking anywhere near Clint, the other two seemed incapable of even meeting his eye. They dragged themselves up by the bootstraps and hobbled away, trying to ignore whatever bumps and bruises they'd been given.

As much as he'd wanted to give them a few parting digs, Clint refrained from letting out so much as a chuckle. The children with the blonde, however, weren't so restrained. The young ones giggled to each other and the boy started to say something to the men before he was stopped by the woman.

The blonde was still putting the children in their places when Clint walked over to get a closer look at them. "Everyone all right?" he asked.

Still wound up tighter than a watch spring, the boy jumped off the bench and stood directly in front of Clint. Looking up at him with wide, bright blue eyes, he said, "That was great what you did, mister! You really showed those two!"

"It was not great," the woman said sternly. "It was violent and uncivilized. We should never resolve our differences that way."

"She's right," Clint said. "But any man that bothers good folks like you in such an uncivilized manner deserves a whole lot worse. Maybe next time someone should tan their hides and toss 'em into a pig sty where they belong."

The little girl had been doing her best to maintain her resolve, but cracked a little smile when she heard that.

The blonde woman sighed and stood up straight so she was on a more adult level when she whispered, "Thank you for that. I just don't want these two to think they can—"

"No need for an explanation, ma'am," Clint gently interrupted.

Just then, a meek little voice drifted up from the bench. "I think we should invite him to supper," the little girl said. When the blonde looked down at her, the girl added, "It would be civilized that way."

"Yes," the blonde said. "I suppose it would. That is, unless this man has any other plans for the evening?"

"He doesn't," Clint said. "And it would be most uncivilized for me to refuse such a kind offer. Don't you agree?" he asked the little girl.

The girl's cheeks flushed, but she nodded quickly before turning away from him and burying her face into the blonde woman's skirts.

"Those men ain't civil," the boy said. "Do you know what he called me?"

"That's enough, Sam," the blonde woman warned.

"He called me a little monkey!"

Clint turned around, hoping to find the three men still screwing up their courage to take another run at him. Even though the dark-skinned boy seemed more upset to be called a noisy animal, Clint knew the insult ran a lot deeper than that. The men were nowhere to be found, however, so the additional lesson in manners would just have to wait.

"That's very rude," Clint said.

Nodding vehemently, the boy said, "It sure is. Monkeys are silly and stupid. I'd rather be a wolf! Or an eagle!"

"How about a mouse?" the girl asked. "At least they're quiet."

"We'd best be on our way," the woman said as she took hold of each child by the hand. "Any longer and you'll have another fight on your hands."

"Maybe I should accompany you," Clint offered. Even though the other three men were out of sight for the moment, he knew better than to assume they were gone for good. Still, he didn't want to worry anyone about it.

Judging by the look on her face, the blonde woman was worried enough already. "You really think that's necessary?"

"Probably. At least let me see you home."

The girl tugged on the blonde's skirts and when the woman bent down to her, she whispered into her ear. When she was done, the girl watched Clint carefully. The Asian slope of her eyes made it look as if she was always smiling. When the girl truly did smile, her eyes made the expression that much more charming.

The blonde huffed about it for a little while, but eventually gave in. "All right," she said. "Dinner won't be ready for a little while, but I suppose you could always come back if you don't feel like waiting around that long."

"I don't mind," Clint said.

"Good," the little boy chirped. "I want to see your gun. Is that a Colt?"

"Sam!" the blonde scolded. "Don't be rude."

"Rude? You didn't even ask the man his name!"

The blonde didn't have a response to that. Realizing that he'd caught her with a valid point, the boy grinned proudly.

"It's Clint Adams," he said, before Sam got a chance to rub it in.

"Madeline Gerard," the blonde replied.

"And I'm Chen," the little girl added.

"There," Sam said. "Now that's good and civilized."

THREE

As they walked, Clint intended to watch for any indication that those men would try to get one last jab in just to prove themselves. Even worse, there was the possibility that they would round up a few more of their ilk to overpower Clint at the first opportunity. Fortunately on both counts, it was a short and uneventful walk to Madeline Gerard's home. She lived in a little house that was situated among a cluster of similar houses on the outskirts of town. The moment they got within a stone's throw of the house, both children broke free and raced to the front door.

"So you're not married?" Clint asked.

Madeline shook her head.

"Then it's just you and the children living here?"

"That stands to reason," she replied.

"I don't mean to pry. It's just that—"

"You're not prying." Madeline stopped and crossed her arms as she watched the children. Sam and Chen had gotten to the front door, tapped it, and immediately scampered toward a sapling that had been planted between that house and its neighbor, in what must have been some sort of game the two were familiar with. "Most folks around here are very friendly," she continued. "It's just that some of them aren't as understanding about my children's situation."

"So those are your children?" Clint asked.

"In everything but blood. I took the first one in when a bunch of Sioux were passing through and most of the family died of fever. Only a little boy was left and I vowed to care for him."

Clint took a look at Sam, who was now protesting loudly at how Chen must have cheated to reach the sapling before him. "That boy sure doesn't look Sioux."

"Oh, he's not. The Sioux came through here just under five years ago. The rest of the first boy's family came along to take him back to his tribe. Since then I've been taking in all sorts of folks when they're in need. My neighbors say I've got a weakness for strays."

"Where do you find them?"

"It's not difficult," she explained. "You always hear about an outbreak of some sickness somewhere or a train accident somewhere else. Wagons roll through and overturn. Someone's wife or husband goes missing. There's always some bit of news like that, but most folks don't concern themselves with who's left. I just offer a warm bed and some hot meals to folks in need. They move along, but there's always another chance for me to help."

"There's always plenty of bad news to go around." Suddenly, Clint winced. "Sorry about that. Slipped out before I could think better of it."

"That's all right. Unfortunately, you're also correct. I like to think we all do what we can to help put out the fires that spring up. I have a big house and plenty of food, so that's what I can give." Turning to Clint to show him a warm smile, she added, "You step in before other fires get started. Thanks again for speaking up for us back when those men were being so rude."

"Rude is a kinder term than I would have used, but you're

welcome all the same. If it's an imposition for me to stay for supper, you can say so and I'll be on my way."

"Weren't you listening?" Madeline asked. "I have a weakness for strays, and I keep extra food in the house."

Clint nodded and walked along with her as she made her way to the porch and sat down upon a swing. "So where did you pick up those two stray pups?"

"Sam's aunt was a baker in town. She passed away, leaving him alone until I can get in touch with some of his cousins that are supposed to live in West Texas. Chen was left at a train station outside of Tombstone. Her mother was murdered. It was a very grisly affair and I haven't had the heart to tell her about it."

"No child should know too many grisly details," Clint said. "There'll be plenty of time for that later."

"Yes, there will," she said softly.

Clint stood his ground and watched the two children play for a while. The show they put on wasn't exactly theater, but it relaxed him in the same way as when he took a moment or two to follow a couple leaves being thrown around by a swirling wind. When his eyes were drawn toward the neighbor's house, he found a withered old face watching him sternly from a window.

"Maybe I should come back later," he said. "Wouldn't want your neighbors to get the wrong idea."

Madeline followed Clint's line of sight to the window. "Oh, don't worry about her," she sighed. "She's always got the wrong idea." Plastering a friendly smile on her face and waving, she shouted, "Hello, Mrs. Beansley."

The instant she realized she'd been singled out, the old woman pulled her face away from the window and snapped the curtains shut.

"You're welcome to stay as long as you like," Madeline told him.

"Actually, I think I may just come back in a while," Clint

said. "I wasn't expecting to stay here for long, so I'll need to put my horse up for the night."

"I've got a little stable out back," Madeline offered.

The longer Clint stayed put, the more anxious he became. "I wouldn't want to impose. Besides, it looks like you've got your hands full with those two."

"You wouldn't be imposing."

"Do you think those three men from the street will stay away for a while?" he asked, letting her know what he was truly concerned about without spelling out even more grisly details.

Madeline shook her head and immediately shifted back into the defensive posture she'd had before, her arms folded across her chest like a suit of armor. "They keep to themselves unless my children and I walk down a main street."

"Yeah, well, I'd like to make certain of that."

"And when you're through hunting for those wretches, should I expect you for supper?"

"The day I turn down a hot, home-cooked meal is the day when you truly know the entire world has gone off-kilter."

FOUR

After retrieving Eclipse, Clint rode through the entire town, searching for any hint that those three men were lurking somewhere, waiting to answer back for the beating they'd received. As he moseyed down the largest streets, he also made himself available for any ambushes that the men felt like setting up. Clint slouched in his saddle and kept his eyelids drooped as if he'd had one too many whiskeys and had forgotten where he was headed. Every one of his senses was at its peak, however, and he was prepared for anything that might be coming his way.

To that end, Clint was almost disappointed when he wasn't allowed to vent all the steam he'd built up inside. The only hint of trouble he spotted was a glimpse of one of the three men as the filthy bugger walked from one saloon and into another. The man averted his eyes and walked away even faster when he caught sight of Clint. After he ducked into a saloon, he didn't come out again.

Clint tied Eclipse to a post outside that saloon and walked in. The place was about half full, which made it easy to pick out where the other man had gone. The fellow stood at the far end of the bar, flanked by the same two assholes who'd joined him in harassing Madeline in the street.

Clint approached the three men and stood near them, leaning with his elbows upon the bar and ordering a beer. Without looking directly at the three men, Clint asked, "You fellas have anything to say to me?"

Just as he'd done earlier that day, the same spokesman was the only one to make a sound. "You talkin' to us?"

"Yeah," Clint replied as he turned to face the three. Not only had the trio not tried to surround him when he wasn't looking, but they pulled back a little when Clint faced them directly.

"What would we have to say to you?" the spokesman asked.

"I don't know. You seemed to have plenty to say to Madeline Gerard."

The moment Clint mentioned that name, he noticed several people within the saloon perking their ears up.

"Do you even know that bitch?" the spokesman asked.

"Easy, Lang," the barkeep warned. "I don't want any trouble in here."

The spokesman nodded and acknowledged the barkeep with a few pacifying waves. "Do you know what she does, mister?"

"Does she murder folks?" Clint asked.

The question obviously caught Lang off his guard. "N- . . .no."

"Does she steal? Is she a horse thief?"

"No."

"Does she hurt anyone or break any laws?"

"Not as such, but—"

The tone in Clint's voice cut Lang off just as sharply as a blade. "Then what the hell did she do to deserve getting shoved around in the street by three assholes like you? The way you were grabbing at her, it seemed pretty obvious that you meant to do a hell of a lot more than that."

"She gives comfort to Indians, Mexicans, killers, and thieves alike," Lang snapped.

"She offers shelter to folks in need!"

"Were you here last spring when them redskins came back to claim the whelps they left behind?" Lang asked.

"Those savages tore apart half the town lookin' for them little brats. When Miss Gerard handed them over, the redskins damn near burned us all out of our homes. Or what about the night when them Texas Rangers rode in looking for some worthless prick wanted for rustling cattle? Were you here when them law dogs faced those rustlers and half a dozen of our friends and neighbors were killed in the cross fire?"

Clint kept his eyes locked on the three in front of him as he replied, "No. I wasn't. Do you mean to tell me that Miss Gerard has anything to do with that?"

"None of them things would'a happened if she hadn't been around to offer herself to every transient that drifts through here. Sorry," Lang added with a filthy grin. "I mean she offers her *house* to them."

"What about you?" Clint asked as he shifted his gaze to the barkeep. "Does everyone around here approve of pushing around ladies and children?"

Reluctantly, the barkeep said, "No, but she does bring a bad kind into this town. We do our best to keep undesirables away from here, but she offers them room and board. Them kids she puts up belong to someone and the folks that come around to claim them ain't always the most charitable kind."

"Is that why no lawmen have come along to speak to Miss Gerard yet?" Although he didn't get a direct answer to his question, he saw enough guilty sneers upon the faces around him to do the job.

After a heavy silence, one of the other men with Lang finally spoke up. "We ain't got anything against kids, but that Miss Gerard ain't what you think she is. She's been warned plenty of times to leave town, but she won't go. Worse than that, she keeps bringing them strays here to attract more trouble that would otherwise pass us by."

"Is that so?"

"Yes, sir," the man replied. "It is."

"The only thing that bitch cares about is them wayward little pups she collects," Lang continued. "You want to find out for yourself? Then go ask the sheriff. He'll tell you."

"I don't need to talk to the sheriff about anything," Clint said. "If Miss Gerard is breaking the law, then she would've already been arrested. That is, unless your town's law doesn't have the gumption to pay a visit to a woman. In the meantime, stay away from her. That goes for you, Lang, as well as anyone else."

Nobody else spoke up, so Clint took a healthy drink of the beer he'd ordered and left.

FIVE

As much as Clint would have liked to discount everything that had been said at the saloon, he still had a little time to kill before supper, and the sheriff's office was on his way to Madeline's house. The little office took up less space than the dry goods store beside it and was only occupied by one man when Clint stepped inside.

"Are you the town law?" Clint asked the young man sitting behind a short desk.

The man looked up, showing Clint a clean-shaven face and bloodshot eyes. "I'm Sheriff Bailey. What can I do for you?"

"Did you happen to know a woman was attacked in the street a little while ago?"

The sheriff stood up and asked, "Who was it? Is she hurt?"

"It was Madeline Gerard."

That was enough to convince the sheriff to take his seat again. "Oh," he grunted. "Her."

"That's right, her. Does she somehow fall out of your jurisdiction?"

"From what I hear, she wasn't hurt. Just called a name or two."

"It was going to be more than that if I hadn't stepped in," Clint said. "What gets under my skin even more is the fact that nobody around here seems to care what happens to Miss Gerard. Some folks seem to think she deserves a lot worse."

"Then she should have brought the situation to my attention," the sheriff replied as he got himself situated behind his modest stack of papers. "I can't exactly know about every little thing that goes on during the day."

"What's she done to deserve so much grief?"

Flinching at the directness of the question that had been posed, the sheriff folded his hands upon his desk and replied, "She tends to attract an unsavory bunch to this town."

"You mean children that don't happen to be from local families?"

"The children aren't the problem," Sheriff Bailey replied. "It's the folks that come around to claim them. And it's not just children she looks after, you know. There have been fugitives from the law as well as a few individuals who were hiding out from a gang known to kidnap anyone with a family rich enough to pay a ransom. That's a particularly rough bunch run by a man named Kyle Morrow. Ever hear of him?"

"I recall the name."

"Then maybe you recall all the men, women, and children he killed when he robbed that Federal Reserve bank in California? Some of those survivors wound up in Miss Gerard's care."

"What's so wrong with that?" Clint asked.

"Nothing, until one of Kyle Morrow's boys came looking for someone he thought might be planning to tell what they knew to the U.S. Marshals. Shot the hell out of this whole town just to find out where Miss Gerard was. Another one of her neighbors was gunned down before me and my deputies showed up."

"Isn't that part of your job, Sheriff?"

Bailey nodded solemnly. "Yes, it is. There's only one problem. Do you see any deputies now?"

Clint took a quick look, which was mostly out of reflex. The office was quieter than an undertaker's parlor, even with the conversation that was taking place. "No, I don't see any deputies."

"That's because they were killed by that gunman who came looking for Miss Gerard," Bailey pointed out.

"Is that her fault?"

"No, sir, it isn't," the sheriff said with a heavy sigh. "But the folks she cares for bring in a dangerous element to an otherwise peaceful town. They gun people down. They set fire to places. One man she sheltered was set to hang for burning down part of a mining camp in the Sierras. He escaped from the lawmen, she sheltered him, and when he slipped away from her he went and set another fire. And those kids she sees to might be little angels, but a lot of them were abandoned because they have good-for-nothing parents, and when that kind comes around looking for their offspring, they tend to get rowdy. Rowdy good-for-nothings bring more trouble. You see where I'm headed with this?"

"Yes, I do. A woman living alone has the audacity to care for children and others in need who are trying to get away from a bad situation. When the cause of those situations comes skulking about, the law and damn near everyone else brand her as a pariah instead of helping to fix the situation before it gets worse."

"My men were killed by an element that she brought here!" Sheriff Bailey snarled.

Instead of backing down, Clint placed his hands on the edge of the lawman's desk, leaned forward, and said, "The whole reason for law is to keep killers and thieves from harming innocents. You'd rather hang a woman like Miss Gerard out to dry instead of actually working for the pay you receive?"

The sheriff had been angry, but that fire was already dying out. "I can only do so much without any deputies."

"All of them were killed?"

"Three out of five," Bailey replied. "The other two quit after seeing their friends slaughtered in the street."

"And what happened to the man who killed your deputies?"

"He shot the woman he was after and rode off. It was the bloodiest day this town has ever seen. Perhaps the bloodiest for the whole county."

"And everyone thinks Miss Gerard brought it on?" Clint asked.

"Whether folks think that or not, they'd be right in saying it wouldn't have happened if she would have left things alone instead of hiding fugitives in her root cellar."

"Fugitives?" Clint scoffed.

Sheriff Bailey nodded. "The woman she was hiding was wanted by the U.S. Marshals for questioning regarding Morrow's whereabouts. Instead of handing her over when the Marshals came, Miss Gerard kept her mouth shut so that fugitive wouldn't have to put the affair to rest. Once that came out, it left a bad taste in a lot of mouths around here."

"I suppose it would."

"So, is there anything else I can do for you?"

There were plenty of things Clint wanted the young lawman to do. But since Bailey clearly wasn't about to step in on Madeline's behalf, he kept those requests to himself. The sheriff hadn't even asked for Clint's name, which spoke volumes as to how much effort he was willing to expend on anyone associated with her.

Clint left the office without another word and Sheriff Bailey didn't lift a finger to stop him.

SIX

When he returned to Madeline's place, the entire house smelled like freshly baked bread. The children were still chasing each other in another room somewhere and Madeline answered the door wearing an apron spattered with gravy and flour.

"Pardon the mess," she said as she stepped aside so he could enter. "It's pretty much always like this when there are little ones about."

"Perfectly all right," Clint replied.

"What's wrong? You look . . . stunned."

"Nothing's wrong. I just feel like I stepped into another man's life." Seeing the perplexed look on her face, Clint shook his head and moved along. "Never mind that. I'm probably just hungry."

"Well, that's good, because I've put together a little bit of everything. Nothing too fancy, but hopefully you'll find something you like."

Clint was mulling over those words when he let his eyes wander up and down Madeline's figure. Even with the messy apron and the tousled mess of blonde hair hastily pulled behind her head, she was still an attractive woman. Her face was naturally pretty in a demure, European way. She had a

long neck that drew his attention down to generous breasts
that she was obviously trying to hide beneath too many layers of conservative clothing. No amount of skirts could de-
tract from the wide curves of her hips, and Clint could only
imagine what her bare thighs and legs might look like.

"Mister Adams?" she asked, snapping him from his little
dream.

Shaking his head, he said, "Please, call me Clint. And I
hope you didn't go through too much trouble, Madeline.
Whatever you put together will be just fine."

"Call me Maddy, and save the rest until you've had a
chance to taste the food. Come on in."

Clint walked in and shut the door behind him. No matter
how friendly Maddy was or how happy the two kids were
to see him again, Clint still felt like an intruder. The house
was just too warm and the people were just too accommo-
dating. Compared to all the time he'd spent in rented rooms
or lying stretched out under the stars, it took a bit of time to
feel like he belonged in a genuine home. But it was all those
smiles that seemed particularly out of place. Compared to
the disgusted scowls he'd been forced to endure a few minutes ago, the friendlier side of the coin was more than a
little jarring.

Fortunately, Clint was able to get over that within the
space of a few minutes. Once Sam started climbing all over
him and Chen waved at him from her hiding spot behind an
old chair, Clint was more than willing to put the rest of the
day behind him.

Supper turned out to be a mix of scraps put together into
a stew, served up with some fresh vegetables, a potato-and-
cheese concoction, and a side of something resembling shep-
herd's pie. Clint took ample portions of everything and had
no reservations about asking for seconds. When he'd finally
cleaned his plate for the last time, Chen hopped up to clear
off the table.

"Don't just sit there, Sam," Maddy said. "Help her."

The little boy rolled his eyes and grumbled a bit, but did what he was told. Within seconds after he'd joined Chen in the kitchen, another bickering match ensued. Since nothing was being broken, Maddy stayed at the table with Clint.

"Thanks for coming back," she said. "The children really like having you around. They've been making up stories about what they think you do for a living. Sam likes to think you're a gunfighter, but Chen is convinced you're a soldier."

"Actually, I'm a gunsmith."

"Really?"

"Now *you* look stunned," Clint chuckled.

"Well, to be honest, I've been going back and forth between Sam and Chen's guesses. It's just that, after seeing how you handled those men earlier today . . ."

Rather than let her flounder any longer, Clint said, "I've been known to take a few other jobs as well."

She nodded and got up to start straightening what the children had left behind. "So, how did you occupy yourself before coming back here? If you were out and about, I guess it's safe to assume you got an earful about me and my strays."

Clint would have liked to deny that, but knew Maddy would have seen through it. Even if the truth could hurt her feelings, he knew that lying to her wouldn't do any better in that regard. "I did hear some things, but I dug around to hear more than a few vicious rumors."

"You did? Why?"

"Because, as you may have already figured out, I've been on the bad end of a few rumors myself."

She blushed and twitched, as if she'd been caught in an embarrassing lie.

"From what I gathered," Clint said, "you've been doing a fine job at helping those in need."

"Did you hear about what happened when those men came looking for the people in my care?"

"Yes, and I can't see how any of what happened was your fault."

"I knew those gunmen were coming," she whispered. "The folks staying with me told me plenty of times. I intended on getting them away from here before there was any trouble, but I was too late and it caused a lot of blood to be spilled."

"I heard about the fire," Clint said.

She winced again as a tiredness crept into her eyes and carved some deep lines into her face. "That was another matter entirely. The young man who started a fire in the Sierras set a fire here, too. He just liked fire. It seemed more like a kind of sickness than anything malicious."

"How'd you manage to get involved with him?"

"He escaped from the lawmen that were taking him to a bigger jail," Maddy explained. "By then, I'd gained something of a reputation for giving shelter to anyone in need. He came to me and I tried to help him. I knew he needed to go back to face his punishment, but I didn't want to hand him over to Sheriff Bailey. He might not have done the young man any harm, but he wouldn't have been able to hold off others who would want to dole out their own vigilante justice. You saw those men for yourself earlier today."

In Clint's opinion, saying that Sheriff Bailey might not have been able to hold off a bunch of vigilantes was much more charitable than saying the lawman wouldn't have been inclined or strong enough to do the job. It seemed Maddy was kind to folks even when they weren't looking. He found that quality to be as rare as it was admirable.

"I was about to take him into Tombstone myself," Maddy explained. "But he got away from me and set a fire. He truly was sick and he was truly sorry for what he'd done."

Clint had seen plenty of men who got a thrill from watching something go up in flames. He didn't know if it was a sickness, but he could tell that Maddy was convinced of that much. For that reason, he was confident in telling her, "Your heart was in the right place. Did you ever think it might be easier on you if you just tried to do things a different way? You could still help folks, but . . ."

"But what?" she asked. "Do it in a way that the whole town agrees with? Conduct my affairs only after going around to make sure my choices are accepted by all the ignorant, smelly fools and wrinkled, pinch-faced prunes that fill this town from the ground up?" Suddenly, Maddy placed her hand over the base of her neck and glanced toward the kitchen. It was quiet in there for a moment, but the children soon commenced their arguing again.

"Sorry about that," she said. "I didn't mean to sound—"

"Perfectly all right," Clint told her. "I met several of those fools today and can't blame you in the slightest for getting your feathers ruffled. I wanted to knock that sheriff upside his head after only talking to him for a few minutes."

Maddy laughed, but seemed a bit ashamed to do so. After composing herself a bit, she said, "I've found it better to go about my business and let everyone else go about theirs."

"Still, it may be a good idea to have someone look out for you until those fools lose interest."

"You're not the first person to say that, Clint. Still, I couldn't impose on you for something like that."

"It seems that you don't keep your guests around for too long. How long will these two be with you?"

"I was going to take the children into Prescott. We're to meet the stagecoach a little ways from here, but—"

"But it'd be easier if I took them," Clint interrupted.

She immediately shook her head. "No. Definitely not. They're in my care and that's a generous offer, but I couldn't just hand them over that way."

"Then what if I escorted you? I could make sure you get to the stage without being pestered by those idiots who met you in the street." Seeing that she was considering this offer a lot more than the first one, he added, "I don't like leaving a job half finished. After seeing those three push you around, I couldn't just let you take your chances with them in the middle of open country."

Maddy was softening a bit, but not quite jumping to accept the proposition.

"You might as well say yes," Clint pressed. "Otherwise, I'll just hang back and follow the three of you to meet that stage anyway. The least you could do is give me some company during the ride."

That brought a smile to her face and she nodded. "That's awfully generous of you, Clint. Thanks. Is there anything I can do to repay you?"

"I hear you've got spare rooms for men with nowhere else to go. I could sleep in one of those or I could make do with the corner of Eclipse's stall."

"I've got plenty of rooms and you're welcome to one. Just don't tell the children you'll be joining us for the ride. If you do that, it'll be impossible for me to get them to lay down for a wink of sleep."

SEVEN

Like most any other house that had two floors, the bedrooms were situated on the top floor while just about everything else was down below. This house had more bedrooms than normal, however, and a couple of them were just off the main sitting room where a mud room or a pantry might otherwise be. Clint was put into that room and was perfectly happy with the arrangement. Compared to most beds found in hotels or boardinghouses, Maddy's was a slice of heaven.

The mattress was thick. The blankets were clean and the sheets still smelled like the warm breezes that had dried them out after they'd been washed. The stage she'd wanted to catch was scheduled to leave in just under a week, which gave them a few more days to kill before making the long ride to the platform. There was another stage rolling through town a few days after that, which would have taken them to Prescott after a longer wait, but Maddy wanted to get Sam and Chen to their families as quickly as possible. Also, the prospect of riding on a stage that could be polluted by some of the less tolerant locals was unattractive enough to justify going out of their way.

Clint spent the first day or two watching the locals to make sure nobody tried to harass Maddy as she went about her daily chores. For the most part, however, those locals were content to simply watch her and cluck their tongues disapprovingly when she led the mismatched children down the street. After a while, he got the feeling that she found it amusing to rattle such delicate sensibilities with something as easy as taking the kids out for a walk.

He also had to admit that Sheriff Bailey was doing a good job of watching out for her as well. More than once, Clint spotted the lawman giving hell to someone who seemed about ready to approach Maddy for the wrong reasons. So, for the most part, Clint didn't have much to do while he was in town. That didn't mean he was anxious to leave.

Sam begged to be taught to shoot and Clint started with the specifics of how to disassemble a pistol, clean it, and put it back together again. That was more than enough to get the boy to take up a less dangerous interest. Chen was learning how to cook, and she spent hours upon hours trying to make something for Clint to sample. If the girl had been a little better at her craft, Clint might have busted Eclipse's back the next time he climbed into the saddle.

Madeline was just happy to have an adult to talk to. It didn't take long for her to come out of her shell, and when she did, she talked to him about everything from plays to literature to different breeds of dogs. It all seemed like a mess to Clint, but her voice was pretty enough that listening to her was anything but a chore. He smiled, nodded, and did his best to continue the conversation. Before he knew it, he was settling in for his last night's sleep at that house. When he pulled his boots off and set them in their usual spot near the door, Clint couldn't help feeling a little low.

The knock on his door was so hesitant that he'd almost thought it was a trick of his ears.

"Yes?"

Half-expecting one of the children to be behind such a little rap upon the door, Clint was surprised when Madeline stepped into his room and closed it behind her. "I hope I'm not disturbing you," she said.

"Not at all. Do you need something?"

She looked away from him while turning toward one of the tables. There, she found something that needed straightening. At least, it was something to keep her hands busy for a few seconds. "We'll be riding out to meet that stage tomorrow. It'll be a long ride."

"Not too bad. It should take the better part of the day, but we'll get there without having to ride in the dark."

"That's just it. Chen and I will get on that same stage. I scrounged up a bit of extra money, which should be enough to get her to her grandparents a little earlier than I'd expected." Smirking, she added, "A few folks around here have owed me money for some time and I think they might have been afraid I'd send you around to collect it."

"You should have told me about those debts," Clint told her in a gruff tone. "I would've happily collected them for you."

"No need. People's imaginations were wild enough to get the job done. Anyway, I'll accompany Chen and Sam on the stage, so there's no reason for you to go any farther than that. I sincerely appreciate you keeping an eye on us. I've done just fine on my own this long, but it's nice to have a man around to . . . well," she added while reaching out to rub Clint's arm, "it's just nice to have a man around."

Clint felt a reaction run all the way through his body the instant she touched him. Every time they'd been together, he'd admired the curves of her body and the way she moved or the way her hair curled around her face. More than once, he'd wanted to reach out and touch her, but had held back. Even now, he didn't want to give in fully to what his instincts were telling him.

"You've thanked me enough," Clint said.

"Then don't take this as another thank-you," Maddy replied. "Take it because I want to give it to you." With that, she placed her hands upon his face and pressed her lips against Clint's mouth.

Wrapping his arms around her, Clint held her close enough to feel the body he'd been admiring for the last few days. Maddy's breasts were warm against him and her hair was every bit as soft as he'd imagined. The longer he kissed her, the better she tasted. When Maddy's body melted against him, she let out a soft, contented sigh that he could feel rustling through her entire body.

Clint moved her toward the bed and laid her down. She pulled him down on top of her and began rubbing a leg along Clint's thigh. The moment he settled onto the bed, Clint heard a creak from the wooden frame. That brought one little detail to mind. "The children are still in the house," he whispered. "What if they come looking for you?"

"They're both upstairs. If they take more than two steps out of their rooms, I can hear the floor squeak anywhere in the house." Grinning, she added, "That's why I put you in this room."

"Ahh," Clint replied as he ran his hands along her body, "that's some good thinking."

EIGHT

Maddy lay back and let Clint undress her. He took his time, peeling off her clothing one piece at a time. The closer he got to her bare skin, the more anxious Clint became. Every one of her dresses covered her beyond a respectable degree. Loosening all of those buttons and sliding his hands up under all those skirts made Clint feel like he was unwrapping the best present under the Christmas tree.

When she was finally naked, Clint stood up to admire the view. She lay sprawled upon the bed with one hand tucked under her head and the other dangling off the edge of the mattress. "Well?" she said. "You'd better not make me wait."

"No, ma'am," Clint replied as he unbuttoned his shirt. He didn't have to wait long before she reached out to help him in his task. Soon, he was naked and sliding under the sheets with her.

From there, Clint placed his hands upon her body and let them roam as his lips found hers in a deep, passionate kiss. Maddy groaned softly and slipped her tongue into Clint's mouth while draping one leg over him. Clint lay on his side, facing her, and then nestled in close. Every breath she took caused her breasts to push against him. When his hands found her fine, rounded hips, Clint slipped them around to cup her rounded backside. Maddy responded to that by scooting in a little closer until his rigid penis brushed against the damp thatch of hair between her legs.

Maddy continued to grind her hips against him. She moved as if she were desperate to feel him inside of her, but was also enjoying the touch of his hardness against her pussy. In the end, Clint was the one to cave in first, and he reached down to guide his cock to where it belonged. He entered her with a gentle push, causing Maddy to pull in a deep, shuddering breath.

Grabbing one of her legs, Clint was able to slide in and out of her a few times while still lying on his side. He could feel her muscles tensing and soon, Maddy pushed him onto his back and impatiently climbed on top of him. After a few minor adjustments, she was straddling him and riding his thick column of flesh.

She grabbed hold of the pillow on either side of Clint's head while straining her entire body to move back and forth on top of him. Clint ran his hands along her sides, savoring the feel of her smooth skin and settling upon the supple curve of her hips. When Maddy straightened up to ride him properly, he cupped her breasts just enough to feel their weight as they swayed to the rhythm of her movements. Before too long, she found the perfect speed and the perfect angle to put a contented smile on her face as she slowly rocked back and forth.

Clint could feel her getting wetter as she continued to ride him. Maddy closed her eyes and leaned her head back before allowing it to droop forward so her hair spilled down to brush against his chest. She swayed as if in a trance, so Clint decided to wake her up again with a slap on her rump that was just hard enough to make a sound.

Her eyes snapped open and she asked, "What was that for?"

He grinned up at her, grabbed her hips, and pumped up into her with one solid thrust. The surprise that had been on her face before was quickly replaced by a jolt of pleasure as he filled her. When she started to say something else, Clint cut her short with another powerful thrust. Maddy quickly gave in to him and leaned down so she could wrap her arms tightly around his neck.

Clint wrapped his arms around her as well, holding her in place as he started to pump vigorously into her. When he sat up, she moved right along with him until they sat facing each other with her legs encircling his waist. They stayed like that for a little while until Maddy started to grow weak. He eased her back so she could prop herself up with her arms stretched out behind her. That way, she faced him with her back arched and her legs spread wide open to accommodate him.

The view from Clint's angle was breathtaking. Maddy's breasts were on full display and her nipples were standing perfectly erect. Both of them ground their hips together so Clint could slide into her like a piston. Between that and the strain of keeping from making any noise, the two of them worked up a sweat that covered their bodies in a glistening sheen. Clint eased out of her and allowed Maddy to lie on her back before she got too worn out.

Keeping one leg propped up, she smiled gratefully as Clint settled in between her thighs and entered her again. "That's better," she sighed.

His erection was rock-solid and eased between the wet lips of her pussy until every inch was buried inside of her. Now that he was on top, Clint could go as fast or slow as he wanted. Maddy moved her hands along his bare chest and rubbed his shoulders while enjoying every second. When Clint lowered himself so he was lying flat against her, she wrapped one leg completely around him while moving the other up and down along his thigh.

"Make it last," she whispered.

Clint brushed her hair away from her face and replied, "Don't you worry. I'm not done with you yet."

She smiled and closed her eyes, trusting him to keep his word.

They explored each other for a while after that. Sometimes, Clint would stay perfectly still while remaining inside of her until she started to squirm or grind against him. When he couldn't hold out any longer, Clint knelt on the bed between her legs. Maddy spread them open wide and reached down to guide him into her again. The moment he found his mark, Maddy responded with an urgent, throaty moan.

The time for tenderness had passed. Every inch of Maddy's body ached for him and Clint wasn't about to hold himself back any longer. He pumped in and out with a rhythm that quickly gathered steam. Maddy turned her head to one side and grabbed the mattress with both hands, her body tensing with every thrust.

Clint grabbed her hips in both hands and drove his cock all the way into her again and again. The bed started to creak beneath them and Maddy was making more and more noise with her insistent grunts. Rather than worry about making noise, Clint gave in to his most primal urge and continued to pump between her legs.

He could feel his climax approaching, so Clint reached down with one hand to rub the sensitive nub of Maddy's clitoris with his thumb. Her eyes snapped open again in an expression of very pleasant surprise. She might have tried to say something, but her next breath caught in her throat as her orgasm immediately pulsed through her. When Clint started to move his hand away, she grabbed it tightly to keep it right where it was.

Rubbing her clit in slow circles, he thrust a few more times until his own pleasure reached its peak. Although Maddy had already been shaking, she shook even more when he exploded inside of her. In fact, she raised her backside up off the bed and watched him intently while desperately trying to draw a full breath into her lungs. When he was spent, Clint lowered her onto the bed and lay down beside her.

"I . . . I've never felt like that before," she gasped.

Clint wiped the sweat from his brow and said, "I can make you feel like that anytime you like."

She rolled onto her side and began tracing her fingertips through the hair upon his chest. "You'd better be able to back up a promise like that."

They didn't have much time, since they both needed to rest up for the next day's ride. Even so, Clint managed to make good on his promise before the sun came up.

NINE

Their bags were already packed, so it was only a matter of loading them onto the horses and getting the kids situated before leaving town. Eclipse carried Clint and Sam, while a bright-eyed dun carried Maddy and Chen. Since all of them knew to travel lightly, they were able to maintain a good pace throughout most of the day.

The stagecoach was to meet them at a platform that was its first stop outside of Tombstone. Barring any unforeseen emergencies, Clint figured they'd arrive there with plenty of time to spare. A small camp had been built up around the platform, offering a place to eat, drink, and sleep if need be. Clint had guessed the children would squirm or put up enough of a fuss to slow down the entire ride by a few hours. As it was, Sam and Chen were content to hold on and sit still for most of the day.

They arrived at the stagecoach platform while the sun was still relatively high in the sky. Even after spotting the structure and the wooden-framed tents surrounding it, Clint had to look around for something else. "Is this the right place?" he asked.

"Sure it is," Sam replied. "Unless you think you got us lost."

"We just got here awfully quick, is all."

Reining her horse to a stop beside Eclipse, Maddy said, "We got here early. How nice!"

"Mister Adams thinks we're lost," Sam said.

Clint twisted around to get a look at the boy. "Not lost, just early."

The boy shrugged, but kept from saying anything else.

The four of them rode toward the platform and tied the horses to a post in front of a water trough that was a quarter full. As soon as their riders had climbed down, both horses began gratefully lapping up the water.

"This is where we part ways," Maddy said. "Thank you so much for seeing us this far."

"I can stay with you until the stage arrives," Clint offered. "I might as well, since I'm here."

Although she seemed ready to refuse, Maddy nodded. "I'm sure the children would like to visit with you for a while longer."

As they walked over toward one tent marked by a sign that read EATS, Maddy slipped her arm through Clint's. They took their time eating a meal of burnt potatoes and tough ham steaks until the stage rattled to a stop near the platform.

"I suppose we should get going," Maddy said.

The children started to put up a fuss and Clint was quick to join in. "They won't be ready to take on any passengers for a while," he said. "They need to unload and water the horses."

"And I bet the drivers need something to eat," Chen offered.

Clint nodded and said, "That's right. There's still some time."

"No, we should go. I highly doubt anyone from town has followed us this far," Maddy pointed out. "Those fools may be persistent, but they're not that ambitious."

"Yeah, you're right," Clint admitted. "I suppose I just

got comfortable around you three." When he took a breath and stood up, Clint felt more like his old self. Actually, he felt as if he'd forced some distance between himself and the three people whose company he'd grown to like. He wasn't about to fool himself into thinking he could settle down into something as comfortable as a little house, a gentle woman, and two little ones, but it was nice to try it on for a while.

What made it even easier was the fact that Madeline had obviously enjoyed their time together just as much.

Taking those few moments to ground himself was enough for Clint to look at the other three in the proper light. He'd taken a shine to the little patchwork family and didn't want to see any harm come to them. That was it, plain and simple. The rest was just trying to hold on to a wisp of smoke.

"You two take care, now," Clint said as he stooped down to the children's level. Both Sam and Chen gave him a hug and then stepped away as if they'd come to the same realization as he had.

Madeline waited her turn and hugged Clint the moment he stood up again. Placing her lips to his ear, she whispered, "If you'd be willing to come back here in a few weeks, I could use an escort back home."

"Just you and me?" he asked.

"Just you and me." When she spoke those last words, she made certain to warm up Clint's ear a bit more with the heat from her breath.

"Tell me when and I'll be there."

This time, Madeline didn't ask if it would be too much trouble for him to come back or if he minded making the trip again. She just gave him a little smile to let him know that she would make it more than worth his while.

TEN

Clint didn't have any problem whiling away a few weeks in Tombstone. There were plenty of old friends to visit, card games to play, and even shows to see. The Birdcage Theater was every bit as colorful as he recalled, and there was even a group of jugglers performing nightly who didn't mind dodging the occasional bullet during their act. When it was time to leave, Clint tacked on an extra day just in case the stagecoach schedule had been thrown off for some reason.

He rode back to the stagecoach platform, where all the same rickety tents were waiting for him. This time, however, he spotted a sign tacked to a post that should have at least given the camp a name. Apparently, the best the founders could come up with was "Express Stop Number 17." Before renting a cot inside one of the tents, Clint tied off Eclipse and walked to the little shed next to the stagecoach platform that was barely large enough to fit the one man who sat inside of it.

"Excuse me," Clint said as he approached the hatbox-sized window that looked into the shed.

The man in there was stick-thin, but could very well have

gotten that way after being cooped up in the wooden container through too many summers. He looked up from his book, lifted his spectacles off the bridge of his nose, and squinted at Clint. "What'd you call me?"

"Uhhh . . . nothing. I wanted to ask if the stage from Prescott was on time."

"It should be arriving in an hour or two. Haven't heard any different."

"Good."

Clint meant to leave, but was pinned to his spot by the scrawny man's gaze. The bespectacled fellow studied Clint intently, moving his beady eyes up and down several times before asking, "Are you Clint Adams?"

When he heard that, Clint reflexively stepped back. "Yes."

"I got a message for you."

"What is it?"

"You'll just have to come here and get it," the scarecrow in the box replied.

As Clint approached the shed again, he felt the hairs on the back of his arm stand up. "How do you know who I am?"

"Someone was expecting you."

Hearing those words come from the fidgety little fellow didn't make Clint feel any better. Seeing the man reach down beneath the window to where a holster or shotgun might be kept didn't do him any favors, either. But when the scarecrow brought his hand up again, it was holding something a lot less threatening than a firearm.

"The woman who left this said you might be coming," the scrawny man explained. "She described you pretty good and said you might show up around this time, asking about the stage from Prescott. This," he said while handing an envelope through the window, "is what she left for ya."

Clint took the envelope, feeling more than a little foolish for getting so worked up in the first place. His other hand was still in the vicinity of his Colt, but Clint dug into his pocket for some money instead. "Here you go. That's for delivering the message."

The clerk snatched the money and muttered, "The lady already paid me to see it got to the right hands, but if you insist . . ."

Clint's name was written upon the front of the envelope in a hasty scrawl that had a feminine quality about it. When he'd moved to a spot where there weren't so many others looking over his shoulder, Clint opened the envelope, removed the letter, and skimmed straight down to the signature. It was from Madeline.

Now Clint felt like an idiot for not having guessed as much right at the start. His only excuse was that it had been a long ride to the platform, but even that didn't seem like enough to cover him. Deciding he didn't need to make excuses anyway, Clint leaned against the post supporting the closest tent and started reading the letter.

Clint,

If you're reading this, that means you're at the platform waiting for me to arrive. You must leave this instant before

"Pardon me," someone asked from the doorway of the tent where Clint was standing. "Are you Clint Adams?"

"Yeah," Clint replied as he continued to read.

Before Clint could take his eyes from Maddy's letter, he felt a gun barrel press against his ribs.

"Start walkin' before your guts see the light of day," the voice snarled.

ELEVEN

Clint didn't take a step.

The only muscles he moved were the ones required to turn his head and get a look at who was threatening him.

The man who held the gun looked to be somewhere in his early twenties. His face was slightly weathered and covered with just enough stubble to obscure his face like a bandanna that had been pulled up over his mouth. He was solidly built and had plenty of muscle upon his frame. Raising an eyebrow, he jabbed the gun into Clint's ribs and asked, "Did you hear me, Adams? I told you to move."

Seeing the fire in the younger man's eyes, Clint started walking. His steps were slow and heavy, however, shuffling over the dirt as if his boots were weighted down. "You know my name, but I don't know yours."

"Tough shit."

Another man chuckled as he fell into step with them. Since he didn't seem surprised by the gun in the younger man's hand and didn't make a move to help Clint, it seemed clear which side he was on.

"Where are we going?" Clint asked.

The younger man shifted so his body kept his pistol mostly out of view from any of the others going about their business at or near the platform. "You'll find out when we get there."

"No," Clint said as he planted his feet. "I'll find out right now."

"Get movin'."

"You can push that gun into my ribs all you like," Clint said. "That won't make it seem like a better idea to go some-place where I can be shot in private. What do you want from me?"

The man with the gun let out a sigh and motioned to his partner. The other one was bigger, but had considerably less muscle than the gunman. A round belly hung over his gun belt with almost enough overlap to hide the buckle. At the first man's signal, he moved around to stand in front of Clint.

Now that Clint was surrounded, the first gunman said, "You're to tell us where to find the Chinese bitch."

Clint only knew one Chinese girl who was connected to both him and the woman he'd come to meet. The very no-tion that armed men would be asking for Chen sparked a fire deep in Clint's innards. "Why the hell would I do some-thing like that?"

"Because we need to have a word with her," the first gunman said.

The fat man chuckled and added, "A word and then maybe a little somethin' else."

That was all Clint needed to hear. Just the lecherous tone in the fat man's voice was enough to send him over the edge. Clint's first move was to reach down for the first gun-man's wrist. He did so with the same speed he might use to draw his Colt from its holster, which was more than fast enough to get to his target before the gunman could pull his trigger.

Once he had hold of the gunman's wrist, Clint twisted the pistol in a half-circle and then angled it sharply to one side. The gunman's finger gave way with a wet crunch, but remained within the trigger guard. Clint reached down with his other hand to grab the pistol from above and trap its hammer before it could drop. From there, all he needed to do was wrangle the gun away from its owner. Considering the pain from his snapped finger, the gunman was more than happy to let the weapon go.

All of this happened in the blink of an eye. By the time the fat man saw what was going on, he barely had time to fumble for his own .44.

Clint got a proper grip upon the gun he'd taken from the first man and then drove its barrel into the second one's ample gut. "What do you want with the girl?"

The fat man sputtered something, but didn't get out more than a few choked syllables before someone else hollered at him from the nearby saloon.

"What's the matter, Jesse?" the man called out from the saloon. "You choke on a chicken bone?"

The first gunman clutched his right hand and shouted, "That's Adams! Put him down!"

Clint turned to find no less than three armed men emerge from the saloon and fan out to form a firing line as they drew their pistols and took aim. In that time, Clint moved around to get behind Jesse and wrap his left arm around the larger man's flabby throat. Tightening his grip around Jesse's neck, Clint looked over the fat man's shoulder at the others. Unfortunately, Jesse was so fat that Clint couldn't do much more than that while using him as a shield. In order to fire a few shots of his own, Clint would have had to lift his gun hand up high and fire downward.

While Clint was trying to figure out what to do with his rotund shield, the three gunmen from the saloon opened fire. Lead whipped through the air over Clint's head and one shot even tore a nasty gouge across the top of Jesse's shoulder.

Hunkering down behind Jesse, Clint drove his knee into the fat man's back and shoved him forward. Jesse waddled toward the gunmen, waving his arms and staggering like a drunken sailor.

"Don't shoot!" the fat man cried.

"Get the hell out of the way!" one of the others shouted.

Clint rushed toward the only cover he could find, which was the little shack near the stagecoach platform. Pressing his back against the wooden structure, he leaned toward the wall and said, "I know you're in there! Who are those men?"

The scarecrow's response was a shaky squawk. "What? How would I know?"

More shots were fired as the gunmen spoke amongst themselves.

"They know my name," Clint said. "The lady who left that letter knew my name and told it to you. I don't know anyone else in this place, so that leaves you."

Just when it seemed the scarecrow was going to keep his silence, a barrage of shots knocked a few holes through his shack. "They didn't ask about you!" he squealed from somewhere close to the floor of the shack. Clint slid down so he was squatting with his back against the wall and his head was closer to where the scarecrow must have been cowering.

"The tall fella asked about the Prescott stage and I asked him the same thing I asked you," the scarecrow continued. "He asked a whole bunch of other questions, which brought him back to the lady who left that letter for you. She's the one he was interested in."

"And they know she wanted to contact me," Clint snarled.

A few more shots blazed past the shack, but the gunmen were easing up on their triggers. In the lull, the scarecrow said, "Yeah, they know. They paid me to keep quiet about it until they got you."

"Who are they?"

"I swear I don't—"

Several more shots were fired from multiple angles. The gunmen must have spread out to surround the shack, because their bullets tore through the flimsy structure and splintered the three walls facing the saloon. Clint hunkered down a bit lower, but knew it would only be a matter of seconds before he was either forced from hiding or killed where he was.

"Damn, Maddy," Clint whispered to himself. "For such a sweet lady, you sure make a lot of enemies."

TWELVE

Since he didn't have a lot of time for a thorough check, Clint hefted the gun he'd taken so he could estimate its weight. He'd spent more than enough years around firearms to know the difference between the feel of a loaded pistol and an empty one. He was confident the young gunman's weapon was probably fully loaded, but he wasn't about to bet his life on it. When he scrambled away from the shack, he took a quick look at the area in front of the saloon.

As he'd figured, just about everyone had run for cover when the shooting started. That left the three gunmen, the one with the snapped finger, and Jesse, to stand out like birds sitting on a telegraph wire. Clint aimed the stolen pistol at them and fired as quickly as he could while continuing to move.

His shots weren't accurate, but they came in a loud firestorm and tested the nerve of all the men in front of him. Even experienced gunfighters would have been thrown off their game by that kind of return fire, but these men were rattled a whole lot more than that. A few of them kept firing but sent their bullets into the street or hissing up toward the clouds. The rest simply scattered.

Knowing he was either out of ammunition or close to it,

Clint tucked the stolen gun under his belt and drew his own modified Colt. "What's this about?" he asked. "Speak up and maybe we can resolve this without anyone getting killed."

"Tell us where to find the Chinese whore and you won't have to get killed," one of the others replied from wherever he was hiding.

Choking back the impulse to shoot that man on principle, Clint said, "What do you want her for?"

The man who stood up was the same one who'd had his gun taken away. Clint had to give the man credit for collecting himself so soon. Of course, it seemed to help that he looked able to pull a trigger with his left hand just as easily as he could his right. He even had another pistol taken from the double rig around his waist to back up his words. "You're outnumbered, mister," he said. "Tell us where that house is before we hurt you bad enough to wish you would've told us the first time I asked."

"I don't know what house you're talking about."

"Sure you do. Didn't you read that letter yet?"

"Nope."

"Then come along with us," the gunman said as his partners slowly stepped out from where they'd hidden. "You'll have time enough to read it along the way."

"The way to where?"

Jesse had been crouching behind a barrel, which hadn't been big enough to fully protect him anyway. Anxious to regain some of the pride he'd lost by getting captured so easily before, the fat man stepped forward and said, "For Christ's sake, Ayden, just shoot the prick's legs out from under him and we'll drag him to the camp!"

That idea was good enough for the rest of the men and the remaining three raised their guns to see it through.

Clint fired three quick shots from the hip, two of which clipped the men who had come from the saloon and sent them to the ground. Before those men hit the dirt, Clint was already running to where Eclipse was tethered. Jesse waddled to follow him, so Clint fired in his direction. The fat man reflexively grabbed the bloody section of his shoulder and dropped. He'd either been hit in the same spot as before or was petrified of that very thing. Either way, he was down for the moment.

After untying Eclipse, Clint climbed onto the Darley Arabian's back and snapped the reins. He then turned and spotted Ayden and one of the men from the saloon taking aim at him. Clint sent a round into the closest one, knocking him off his feet with a solid hit to the chest to land heavily beside Ayden.

Putting one gunman down kept the others busy for a few seconds, which was all the time Clint needed to ride away from the camp and platform. Gunfire erupted from behind him, but it only added some fuel to Eclipse's fire. The Darley Arabian galloped away amid a cloud of dust and it was all Clint could do to hang on.

Every so often, Clint glanced over his shoulder to look for any trace of a pursuit. The gunmen might have gotten to their horses to try and catch him, but all Clint could see was a few specks on the horizon. After another few minutes, he couldn't even see that much.

THIRTEEN

Clint took a roundabout way back to Madeline's house, just in case those gunmen were still following him. He circled and doubled back a few times before even truly getting halfway back to her town. From what he'd heard, those men didn't even know where to start looking for her home, but Clint took those extra precautions to make certain of it. Between his backtracking and Eclipse's natural speed, they never got close enough to any pursuers for Clint to catch sight of them.

Once he got close enough to the town to see it, Clint pulled back on his reins and removed the spyglass from his saddlebag. A careful study of the terrain behind and around him revealed nothing but a few coyotes and one wagon making its way into town. After dropping the spyglass back into the pack, Clint took Maddy's letter from his pocket and read it all the way through.

Clint,

If you're reading this, that means you're at the platform waiting for me to arrive. You must leave this instant before you're seen. There are men after me and they might hurt you if they know you're a friend of mine.

"Too late for that," Clint chuckled. He shifted in his saddle and continued reading.

> *Sam and Chen are safe, but I've acquired another one of my cherished strays. I call her Lylah, but I'm not certain what her true name is. Because of my current circumstances, I arranged for Lylah to arrive at my house before me. That way, I hope to prevent any trouble with the same men who have forced Lylah into my care.*
> *I know it's a lot to ask, but I implore you to go to my house and make sure Lylah is all right. I hope to be there to meet you, but if not, you'll need to make sure she gets to the proper authorities. She has information about a killer named Kyle Morrow. If you're unable to come back to my house, please get this information to someone who can help. I fear the local law isn't quite up to the task.*
>
> *Maddy*

Clint smirked at the thought of just how much he agreed with that last sentence. From what he'd seen of Maddy's local law, it wasn't quite up to the task of tossing drunks. Protecting anyone from a known killer seemed to be way too much trouble for someone like Sheriff Bailey. As Clint folded the letter and placed it back into his pocket, he realized that the gunmen at the stagecoach platform might not have been referring to Chen after all.

Without letting another moment slip by, Clint tapped his heels against Eclipse's sides and rode into town. He didn't stop at the sheriff's office and didn't waste a second in looking around at the folks on either side of the street. Nobody was shooting at him and, as far as he could tell, nobody was following him. Everything else was beneath his notice.

Upon arriving at Maddy's house, Clint drew his pistol and circled the place. His eyes darted up and down, side to side, looking for anyone peeking from a window or waiting in any kind of possible ambush. There was no one on the roof and not so much as a hint of movement that he could see. Bringing Eclipse to a halt at the back of the house, Clint dismounted and carefully approached the back door.

It wasn't until that moment that he realized just how long he'd gone without taking a slow breath. The stagecoach platform was a sizable distance away, but Clint had covered it in record time. Although Eclipse did most of the work in that regard, Clint's muscles were feeling the strain of being in the saddle for so many hours without letting up on his pace. To go along with the physical strain of making such a rushed journey, being ready for a fight or watching for an ambush for all of that time took a toll of its own. Clint's blood raced through his veins. His breath came in shallow gulps. His muscles all felt as if they'd been drawn taut and stretched thin over his bones. Even his eyeballs felt as if they'd spent the day rattling around in their sockets.

Standing with one foot propped against the step leading up to the back door, Clint filled his lungs and let out his breath in a steady sigh. It didn't relax him completely, but at least the rushing in his ears died down enough for him to hear a bit more than his own heartbeat. And then, to set his whole system to running again, Clint slammed his shoulder against the door and pushed it open.

He jumped into Maddy's kitchen with his gun in hand. Although he could still hear the echo of splintering wood, he could tell the entire house was a bit too still for its own good. His instincts had been to come in like a bull rather than take his chances announcing his presence with a polite knock. Stalking forward into the familiar home, he could tell those instincts had been correct.

The house didn't feel the way it had when he'd left it.

The air was thick and had the feel of a tomb.

But there was something more than that. Clint could sense something on an animal level that caught somewhere between his nose and his brain. It was something that let him know he was being watched, mixed in with a liberal dose of fear. More often than not, those things hinted at an ambush. He could be wrong about that, but Clint wasn't going to be caught unaware.

"Maddy?" he called out.

There was no response.

"Maddy? It's Clint."

Still nothing.

Clint set his sights upon the doorway leading from the kitchen to the dining room. Just as he was stepping through, the ambush he'd been waiting for finally arrived. And, despite all his preparation and jangling nerves, the damn thing still caught him by surprise.

FOURTEEN

There really wasn't much to see in the kitchen. Apart from the stove, several cupboards, and the table where Maddy did most of her cooking preparation, there were only a couple of stools scattered throughout the room. Since nobody could really hide behind one of those stools, Clint had moved along. Unfortunately, someone could hide in one of the cupboards. Clint discovered that the hard way when a wild banshee exploded from the cupboard where it had been hiding to swat furiously at Clint's back and arm.

Clint wheeled around and swung his arm reflexively at whatever was attacking him. Since none of the blows had really hurt him, he only swung his arm at about half its strength. His effort didn't matter either way, since the banshee easily ducked under it to start kicking his shins. Unlike the first round of attacks, those kicks hurt.

"Hey!" Clint yelled as he backed away. "What the hell?"

He held his gun in hand, but had yet to get a clear look at his target. When he tried to move away, he merely caught another batch of kicks in a different spot. The banshee looked to be about the size of a small woman, but was hunched over to the height of a child. Long, straight black hair hung down to cover the banshee's face. The arms and legs that continued to batter Clint were thin, but strong enough to do some damage.

Since he wasn't about to shoot the banshee just yet, Clint grabbed the first body part he could reach that wasn't flailing too much to be caught. Once he closed his fist around a clump of hair, he pulled the banshee away and stepped back.

The banshee looked up at him and bared its teeth. Despite the twisted features and sweaty skin, it was obviously the face of a woman.

"Who are you?" Clint asked.

The woman looked to be somewhere in her late teens or early twenties. Before Clint could see much more than that, she snarled and reached up to sink both sets of fingernails into the hand that had grabbed her hair. She growled viciously as she drove her nails in deep enough to start a trickle of blood flowing down from Clint's hand.

"Ow, son of a—" was all Clint could say before a kick landed squarely on his shin. He'd been about to let her go before, but he sure as hell let go of her now. The instant she'd hopped back a step, the banshee stood up straight and delivered a solid kick between Clint's legs.

A wave of cold flowed up from Clint's privates and flooded into his stomach. He tried to pull in a breath, but could only draw enough air to let out a hacking wheeze. He reached down to hold on to the spot where he'd been kicked, knowing all too well what was coming next. Sure enough, the pain exploded in him a few seconds later. It erupted in a white-hot torrent that went straight up to his spinal cord.

Clint's first instinct was to grit his teeth and beat to a pulp whoever had caused that very distinctive pain. His fist tightened around his Colt and his gaze fixed upon the wild, panicked eyes of the woman in front of him. Although he choked down the bloodthirsty impulse triggered by the pain, enough of it must have shone through in his eyes to put the fear of God into the scraggly young woman.

The banshee spun toward the doorway and ran into the dining room.

"Wait," Clint croaked. He tried to run after her, but wasn't able to get up to full speed. The banshee's legs and feet might have been slender, but they'd hit him with a sharp impact that Clint knew he would be feeling for a long time.

She bolted from the kitchen in a flurry of scrambling limbs and wild hair. Her breaths were short and choppy, filling the otherwise empty house like moans from a ghost.

Clint dragged himself toward the dining room. It took a couple of fumbling attempts, but he managed to drop his Colt back into its holster. Still grabbing himself in his tender nether regions, he grunted, "I'm . . . a friend of Madeline's. She sent me . . . here."

The banshee didn't respond to that in the slightest. In fact, she seemed to have been thrown into a tizzy as she yelped and sent a bunch of heavy objects smashing to the floor. By the time Clint made it to the front room, he found her climbing back to her feet after tripping over a footstool.

Sucking in a breath, Clint pushed as much of it as he could behind his voice. When he spoke, his words sounded almost as feral as the wild woman looked. "I put my gun away. See?" he held out his hands to show her they were empty.

The banshee looked at him and froze.

FIFTEEN

As she stood there in front of him, the banshee seemed to be contemplating whether she was going to bolt for the front door or take another run at Clint.

"My name's Clint Adams. Are you Lylah?"

The banshee's head pulled back and she studied him carefully.

Clint nodded, but didn't take a step toward her and kept his hands away from his holster. "Madeline Gerard brought you here, didn't she?"

Now that the young woman didn't have her hackles up, she looked less like a wild animal. Her eyes widened a bit so they were no longer angry slits. Although they were very pretty and very, very green, those eyes were still frightened.

"Did Madeline tell you about me? Did she mention that Clint Adams might be coming here?"

The woman's eyes darted from Clint's face, to the holster strapped around his waist, and then to the Colt that hung at his side.

"Don't worry," Clint assured her. "If I didn't shoot you after you kicked me in the stones, I won't shoot you now. Why don't I just put this away?" When he slowly inched his hand toward the Colt, Clint could see her eyes widen.

"I'm not going to shoot," he said again. "I'll just toss my gun away so you won't have to worry about it. Would that make you feel better?"

She wasn't about to answer the question. The woman was staring at the gun so intently that she didn't even seem to hear what Clint was saying. The terror in her eyes didn't ease up in the slightest until Clint finally took his hand away from the holster altogether.

"All right," Clint said. "I'll leave the gun where it is. But see for yourself," he added as he held his hands up high. "I'm not going to shoot you."

The woman's brow furrowed, but her shoulders dropped as if she'd just let out a breath that she'd been holding.

Patting the air in front of him, Clint said, "That's better. Why don't we both just sit down and stop all this running?" Knowing there was a chair behind him, Clint reached back for it and sat down. When he bent at the waist, a fresh batch of pain shot through his groin to give him the impression that blood might be trickling down his leg. Getting hit in the family jewels wasn't exactly a fun experience, but it wasn't a new one either. He clenched his jaw and lowered himself onto the chair, praying the pain would let up sooner rather than later.

The woman watched him carefully. As Clint shifted to try to find a comfortable spot in his chair, she flinched with what might have been a touch of sympathy pain. Well, as sympathetic as any woman could get, considering the situation.

"See?" Clint grunted. "We can relax and have a friendly talk. I'm Clint." When he didn't get a response from her, he stretched out his hand.

The woman twitched and backed away.

"Go on and shake it," Clint said as he waggled his hand a bit.

It took a few seconds, but the woman eventually approached his hand the way a curious mouse might approach a piece of bread that had fallen onto the floor. When she reached out to grab his hand, she still looked like a mouse snatching that same crumb.

There was strength in her grip, but the greeting was short-lived. "There," Clint said. "Nice and friendly. Are you Lylah?"

The woman's eyes brightened when she heard that name.

"That's you, isn't it? Hello, Lylah."

Hearing the name again soothed her, telling Clint that the name was something more than just another word to her.

"Has anyone else been here?"

No response from Lylah, but Clint picked up on something in the way she studied him. She watched his mouth when he talked and scowled as if she were trying desperately to see something that just wasn't coming through. Considering the tussle they'd had and how well she'd darted from room to room, Clint doubted she had any trouble seeing. That left one other obvious alternative.

"Can you hear me?" he asked. He got the same amount of nothing from her, so he lowered his voice and kept from moving his lips very much when he spoke her name again. She perked up and studied him closer, which told him that she'd heard his voice well enough to pick out her name.

"Can you understand me?" Clint asked.

She watched him carefully, but only seemed to become more confused.

"Lylah, if you can understand what I'm saying, just tell me. You can stop me at any time, but we need to go." To test the waters a bit more, he added, "I've got friends coming by to burn this place down and then take our banana peels into the waterwheel caboose."

She continued to study him with the same amount of intensity as she had before.

Clint cursed under his breath, realizing that she didn't comprehend much of what he was saying. Leaning forward onto the edge of his chair, he clasped his hands and spoke a

few simple phrases in Spanish, French, Chinese, and a few
Indian dialects he'd picked up throughout the years. He
wasn't exactly fluent in all those languages, but he knew
enough to say howdy to folks who were. Unfortunately, none
of those languages struck a nerve with Lylah. In fact, the
more languages he tossed out, the more confused she got.

"All right, we'll stick to English. Do you know Maddy?"
When he saw the vague hint of a spark in her eyes, Clint
asked, "Madeline. Do you know Madeline?"

Suddenly, Lylah nodded.

Clint felt as if he'd just discovered the wheel. "All right!
Now we're getting somewhere. Where is Madeline? Where . . .
is. . .Madeline?"

It didn't take long for Clint to feel like an idiot for thinking she would comprehend his language better if he slowed
it down. She didn't understand him before and the speed of
his pronunciation didn't help matters any.

She pulled her hair away from her face and blinked
quickly, as if trying to clear some dust from her eyes. Now
that she wasn't snarling at him, Lylah was actually pretty.
Her skin was lightly colored, but not enough to make her
lineage clear. She had the rounded nose and lips of an Indian but the narrowed eyes of an Asian. The lines of her face
were smooth and elegant, leading to a slim neck and narrow
shoulders. Her trim body was wrapped in a buckskin dress
that hugged pert breasts and slender hips. Judging by the
muscles of her legs, she probably walked more than she
rode a horse. Either that, or she just happened to have very
nice legs.

Having spent some time with a few tribes who didn't
speak his language, Clint locked eyes with her and used the
only tools at his disposal. "Madeline . . . where?" When he
said that last word, Clint raised his eyebrows, held up his
hands to either side, and turned back and forth as if he was
looking for something.

"Madeline?" Lylah asked.

Clint nodded, but raised his eyebrows more. "Where?"

She scowled, but not in an angry way, when she asked, "Clint Adams?"

Clint nodded earnestly. Then, he reached into his pocket and took out Maddy's letter. Showing it to her, he said, "See?"

Lylah's eyes widened and she smiled for the first time. It was a very pretty sight. She dug into the pocket of her dress and spoke in a steady flow of words that made as much sense to Clint as his words had made to her. He listened to her carefully, however, to see if he could narrow down what sort of language she was speaking. It sounded Asian, but not Chinese. It wasn't Japanese, either, but that was only going off a few encounters he'd had with people from that area. Lylah's words had an Asian lilt with a bit more of an edge to them. Before Clint could figure out more than that, he was presented with another letter.

She handed it to him and Clint took it. No comparison was necessary for him to recognize the handwriting as Maddy's. It read:

Wait for Clint Adams. Go with him. Hide until he gets there.

The note had been hastily scribbled and, by the looks of it, had been crumpled up more than once.

"Go where?" Clint asked. When he saw the confusion start to spread on her face, Clint pointed to the second sentence of the letter and made the same exaggerated shrug he'd made earlier. "Go . . . where?"

It seemed Clint's efforts had paid off. Lylah understood him well enough to answer with some gestures of her own. Pointing toward the door, she started to wave in a series of several shooing motions.

"Go away from here, huh? That's not a bad idea."

Suddenly, footsteps rattled upon the front porch and some-one started knocking upon the door. Hearing that, Lylah swung her hands toward the back door and waved furiously toward that exit instead.

SIXTEEN

Clint not only agreed with Lylah's idea, but was already seeing it through when the knocks grew stronger and louder. He pulled himself up from his chair, grunting at the fierce pain that still lingered below his belt. Choking back the discomfort, Clint headed for the kitchen and the back door that he'd used to get into the house. Lylah moved like a cat, shooting past him and streaking into the kitchen.

"Hello?" someone said from the front porch. "Is that you, Maddy?"

Clint stopped and looked toward the front door. There was a narrow window near it, but that was covered with curtains. Although he couldn't see who was outside, Clint could tell there was more than one person there.

"I heard a commotion in there," the person said. "Is someone hurt?"

When Clint looked into the kitchen, he saw Lylah motioning at him to hurry up and get through the back door. He held out a hand in a way that said "stop" in nearly every language.

After he'd waited there a few more seconds, Clint heard, "I know someone's in there. Are you all right, Miss Gerard?"

Grudgingly, Clint approached the door. He knew it was either that, or wait to be discovered by the already curious neighbors when he rode away. Lylah didn't like that much at all, and she looked ready to bolt. Before she did that, Clint turned toward her and used one of the words from Maddy's letter.

"Hide."

She knew that one and scampered toward the cupboard where she'd been hiding when Clint first arrived. After the kitchen was quiet again, Clint opened the front door to find the pinch-faced old woman who lived next door standing on the porch along with two young men wearing badges.

"Oh," the old neighbor said. "It's you, Mister Adams."

"Yes, it is."

"Was there a problem? I heard a crash." Leaning to try and get a peek into the house, she added, "Several crashes, as a matter of fact."

Clint winced painfully, which wasn't an act. "Yeah, that was me. I tripped over a chair."

"Is Madeline in there with you?"

"No," he replied, figuring it was safer not to underestimate the old woman's nosiness. "She isn't."

"Who is? I thought I saw a young woman slip in a while ago. Would that happen to be another one of those poor, unfortunate souls Maddy insists on collecting?"

Clint couldn't decide which left a worse taste in his mouth: the way the old woman spoke about Madeline as if she were a friend or the way she crinkled her nose while speaking, as if the words themselves gave off a sour stench.

"There was a young woman in here, but she's already gone," Clint said.

The deputy standing to the old woman's left looked to be in his late twenties, which would put him a few years ahead of the other one on the porch. He stepped forward like a bull demanding entrance into the proverbial china shop. "Where did she go?"

Clint stood in front of the deputy, making it clear he wasn't about to move. "I don't know."

"Then how do you know she's gone?"

"Because she isn't here," Clint said sternly.

"How about we take a look around?"

"Now why would I allow something like that?" Although he enjoyed seeing the dazed look on the deputy's face, Clint added, "This isn't my house. I don't know if the proper owner would approve of having strangers in without permission."

The old woman let out one, coughing grunt of a laugh before saying, "Plenty of strangers drift in and out of this house and she doesn't seem to mind one bit."

Clint responded with, "Maybe, but they have permission."

It wasn't exactly what he'd wanted to say to the shriveled old prune, but it did the trick. She flicked her eyebrows up and backed away. The older of the two deputies was more than happy to stand in her place.

"Are you going to let us have a look in there or do we need to get the sheriff?"

"You go ahead and get the sheriff," Clint said. "Maybe by the time you get back, I'll have a nice little welcome ready for him."

"Is that a threat, mister?"

"Not hardly. I was thinking more along the lines of some water or lemonade. I'm sure there's something to drink floating around in here."

"So all the commotion was on account of you tripping on something?"

"Yeah. It was a chair. If you don't believe me, perhaps this fine lady can verify my story? I'm sure she peeks into enough windows for the odds to be good that she saw me take my spill."

The old woman sputtered and flapped a hand over the base of her throat. While the display was surely meant to show offense, the embarrassed flush in her cheeks and the darting of her eyes spoke to the validity of Clint's claim.

"You'd best step aside and let us take a look in there," the deputy warned.

Before he could think better of it, Clint snapped, "Or what?"

Both lawmen placed their hands upon the grips of their holstered pistols. "Or we'll drag you outside the hard way."

"What's the cause for all of that?"

"Seeing as how Miss Gerard ain't nowhere to be found but one of her troublemaking little stray dogs and a known gunman are in her house is cause enough. Miss Gerard has already brought fire and lead to this town, so it's only fitting that we check up on whatever crawled into her home while she's away."

"I'm the only one here, Deputy," Clint said.

"Then you won't mind if we step in to make certain of that."

Clint pulled in a deep breath, weighed his options, and finally decided upon the one to end the conversation the quickest. "No," he said, hoping Lylah was good at staying hidden. "Come on in and have your look."

SEVENTEEN

The deputies stepped into the house, eyeing Clint as if they expected him to make a move for his gun at any moment. When Clint merely let them pass, the two younger men started glancing about. Clint had already picked out the bigger of the threats and did his best to keep those sharper eyes away from the kitchen.

"So," he said to the nosy old neighbor, "would you like me to have Maddy stop by to say hello when she gets back?"

"No. That won't be necessary," she muttered. Somehow, possibly due to some sixth sense acquired by an old woman who insisted on knowing everything that went on outside her window, the neighbor was drawn to the kitchen.

Acting as if he was clearing a path for the deputies, Clint stepped in front of her. "Weren't Sam and Chen a hoot?"

"Who?"

"The boy and little girl that were here before," Clint said. "Weren't they a hoot?"

"I suppose so. They were certainly noisy."

"Oh, so you heard them squabbling all the time?"

"Most definitely," she groaned.

"And why didn't you come knocking on her door with the law in tow back then?" Clint asked. "I suppose you peeked through a window, snuck over a fence, or otherwise stuck your nose where it didn't belong to make sure it was warranted to bother the sheriff?"

That struck a little too close to home. The old woman glanced toward the lawmen and then cast her eyes toward the floor. "Perhaps I should just go," she said. "It seems you men have enough on your plate already."

"Yes, we sure do," Clint said dismissively. "Bye, now."

After the neighbor was gone, Clint made his way to where the deputies were. One of them was looking in the room where Clint had slept and the other was going toward the kitchen. Needless to say, Clint was more interested in following the latter.

"So, you're looking for what, exactly?" Clint asked.

"Already told you," the deputy replied.

"You didn't tell me much, apart from some trouble that was caused some time ago. You think you'll see a bunch of outlaws huddled in a corner or some child who doesn't strike you as the kind you want in your perfect little town?"

"Yeah," the younger deputy grunted. "That's just what I'm lookin' for."

"Well, I don't see the likes of that in the kitchen. Do you?"

The deputy stopped at the doorway leading into the kitchen. "No, but the back door's open. Were you plannin' on skinning out of here?"

"I was planning on leaving, yeah," Clint admitted. "My horse is right outside. Then I heard the knocking at the front door and decided to answer it. Are you disappointed I wasn't acting more like the bad element you and your sheriff so desperately want to snuff out?"

The deputy walked toward the back door and glanced outside to where Eclipse was waiting. All the while, Clint looked at the cupboards for any trace of Lylah. He couldn't see anything right away. If he didn't know exactly what to look for, he would have completely missed the subtle hint of movement to be seen through the crack of one of the bottom cupboards near the stove.

"What's the matter, deputy?" Clint asked. "You waiting for a bribe?"

The young lawman took the bait perfectly. He stood toe-to-toe with Clint and said, "If you know what's good for you, you'll shut your damn mouth right now! Got that?"

"Sure."

"Good. Now let us do our duty or we'll toss you out of this house with the rest of the trash."

With that, the deputy turned and marched out of the kitchen. Once he was gone, Clint stooped down next to the cupboard where he'd seen the flicker of movement. He opened the door a crack and found Lylah huddled all the way against the back. The bottom half of the cupboard was one large space and had enough shadows to hide the slender young lady almost completely even with the door open.

"Where's Madeline?" Clint whispered.

Having heard the question enough times already, Lylah waved toward the back door.

"We'll go?"

Once again, Lylah proved to be familiar with the words that were in the letter and she nodded eagerly while climbing out. She made it as far as the cupboard door before glancing nervously toward the dining room.

"I can hear them stomping upstairs," Clint sighed. "Let's find Maddy before they do."

As soon as they were outside, Lylah headed for Eclipse.

"Wait," Clint said as he grabbed her arm. "We have to ride?" Seeing that she didn't understand, he asked, "Where?"

Lylah pointed to Eclipse and started speaking in whatever language she knew. All she needed was her hands, however, as she pointed Eclipse and then waved toward the edge of town.

"Far away?" Clint asked.

She kept waving, as if motioning toward a train that was fading into a memory as it sped along the tracks.

"Damn." Pointing to the back of the house, Clint said, "Wait. Hide."

She nodded and found a spot to crouch between the house and a wood pile.

The deputies rummaged through the second floor for a bit before stomping down the stairs. As they headed toward the front door, they found Clint waiting for them in the dining room. While he was more than happy to see them go, he wanted to keep up the banter he'd already started. "Find anything while searching through her knickers?" he asked.

"No," the older deputy replied. "We'll bring back the sheriff to have a word with you."

"Sure you don't want to stay and chat?"

"Yeah."

The deputies slammed the front door behind them and Clint slipped out through the back.

EIGHTEEN

Plenty of questions raced through Clint's mind as he rode Eclipse toward the edge of town.

Was Maddy all right?

Did anything happen when she and Lylah were separated?

How far away was Maddy?

Was anyone after Lylah?

Did anyone see her slip into Maddy's house?

The more he thought about those questions, the more questions sprang into Clint's mind. Unfortunately, the one person who could answer them at the moment could understand less than a dozen words of English.

Clint rode down the streets quickly enough to get away, but not fast enough to make it look like he was running away from a bank robbery. He didn't see Sheriff Bailey or recognize any of the deputies, but that didn't mean the law was oblivious to what he was doing. Rather than stop and try to talk to Lylah, he decided to worry about the situation with the law first and foremost.

Keeping his head down and his eyes facing forward, Clint flicked his reins to get Eclipse moving a bit faster. The streets were widening by now and would soon turn into trails or simply end. The street Clint was on happened to be one of the former, and he waited until open country was in front of him before touching his heels to Eclipse's sides. The Darley Arabian responded right away and went from a trot to a gallop.

Lylah wrapped her arms around Clint's midsection and held on tightly. She pressed her face against his shoulder as the wind whipped around both her and Clint. Her long hair tickled Clint's cheek, putting the scent of wildflowers into his nose. He wondered if that scent was from a bottle or if it was her own, but kept that question to himself, along with the others.

Before going too far, Clint pulled back on the reins and steered Eclipse sharply away from the trail. He came to a stop, but Lylah kept moving up and down as if she were still being bounced by a running horse.

She stretched her arm out so Clint could see her pointing at the trail ahead. As she did, she spoke in a hurried bunch of words that he didn't understand in the slightest. He would have had to be deaf to be ignorant of the fact that she was scolding him for stopping and was insisting that they keep moving.

"I know, I know," he said while waving over his shoulder.

She didn't like that at all and slapped his hand away.

In an odd sort of way, Clint liked that. It was a reaction he would have expected from anyone with a little fire in their belly, and it was something he could understand. "I'm just checking to see if anyone's following us," he said, despite the fact that there was no reason to believe she understood him.

"Was anyone following you?" he asked. Turning to look at her, he said, "Was . . . anyone . . . following . . . ?"

The moment he could see her face, Clint knew what she was thinking. For the most part, the narrowed eyes, furrowed brow, and curled corner of her mouth said she thought he was an idiot for once again expecting her to comprehend his language just because he slowed it down. Clint was embarrassed to admit he agreed with her.

"Sorry," he told her. "Force of habit, I guess." After that, he twisted in his saddle and turned Eclipse in a slow circle so he could survey his surroundings on all sides. It didn't take long before Lylah caught on and began studying the terrain herself.

When he felt a tap on his shoulder, Clint looked back and saw her pointing toward a rider in the distance. She rattled off a few more words, and when he didn't react, she repeated the gibberish in a slower, more deliberate tone.

Clint rolled his eyes and reached into his saddlebag. "Let me have a look," he grumbled. The spyglass he carried did a good enough job in magnifying the image of the other rider, but didn't do much to make up for the darkness of the hour. "I don't think we need to worry about that one," Clint said. When he glanced back to see the unchanged expression on Lylah's face, he waved at the distant rider dismissively and put his spyglass away.

Lylah didn't relax all the way, but she seemed to get Clint's meaning.

"Now, which way do we go to meet—" Stopping himself in mid-sentence, Clint asked, "Madeline. Where?"

Lylah pointed to the trail she wanted him to take. Of course, it wasn't the trail he'd picked on his own. At least their predicament allowed Clint to grumble all he wanted without fear of offending Lylah. Judging by the muttering coming from behind him, she was doing the same.

NINETEEN

They rode well past the time when Clint would normally stop for the night. After he'd gotten onto the proper trail, Lylah settled in behind him and rested her head upon his shoulder. The shadows were thick after nightfall, but the half-moon was bright enough to cast a pale glow upon the terrain. Since they were covering a flat expanse of rocky trail, Clint was confident enough to put some more distance between himself and Sheriff Bailey.

When the trail took on some more twists and turns, Clint pulled back on the reins and stood up in his stirrups. Lylah must have dozed off, because she jumped a bit at the sudden awkward movement of her headrest.

"We should stop for the night," he said to himself more than her. Rather than try to explain, Clint steered for a good spot to make camp. Lylah accepted the hand he offered, climbed down from the saddle, and stepped back so Clint could do the same.

From there they went through the motions of putting together a fire and laying out Clint's bedroll without a word passing between them. They actually got done quicker than Clint had expected, since they simply did what needed to be done rather than waste time talking it over.

Clint warmed up some beans and served them with a side of jerked buffalo. It wasn't the best supper, but neither of them was about to complain. "So," he said while digging his letter from Maddy out of his pocket, "can you read this?"

Lylah set her tin plate down and took the letter. Holding it closer to the firelight, she let out a troubled breath and concentrated upon the words. Every so often she nodded, but mostly she fretted and shook her head.

"What can you read?" Clint asked. He found that he got more results by speaking just a bit slower, but accenting his words with more facial expression than he would normally use in a conversation. He stopped short of playacting, which at least conveyed the general idea or emotion of what he was saying.

The frustration on her face was plain to see and was only intensified when she tried to answer Clint's question. Although it looked as if she wanted to throw the letter into the fire, she handed it back while sighing and shaking her head some more.

Clint pointed to Maddy's signature until he saw that Lylah understood. From there, he pointed in the general direction they'd been riding. "How much farther?" he asked. "How far?"

Lylah looked back and forth and then said, "Tomorrow."

Surprised by the sound of her voice, Clint pointed to Maddy's name again and asked, "Tomorrow?"

She nodded.

"Well then, I suppose that's what I wanted to know."

Lylah seemed to be growing accustomed to Clint rambling on without expecting an answer, because she idly prodded the fire with a stick.

"Thanks."

Clint glanced around as if the word had actually been a bird call or some other trick that had been played upon his ears. When he looked over at Lylah, he found her looking directly at him. The firelight softened her features and gave her skin a vaguely golden hue. Now that the wind wasn't tossing her hair in every direction, it hung on either side of her face like a thick curtain of black velvet.

Once she had his undivided attention, she looked straight into his eyes and said, "Thanks."

"You're welcome."

The smile that came to her face was tired, but showed that she understood what he'd just told her.

Clint took the opportunity to press his luck by asking, "Where are you from?" When he saw the confusion upon her face, he pointed to her and asked, "Where?"

Lylah was even more confused once the question sank in. Looking down at the ground and back up at Clint. "Where . . . is Lylah?"

Seeing where this was headed, Clint shook his head and waved the question off as if he was erasing it from a chalkboard. He picked up his own tin plate, scooped up some beans, and shoveled them into his mouth.

"Tombstone," she said.

"What?"

Lylah waved in the same direction Clint had waved earlier, which was also the direction they'd been riding. "Tombstone."

"We're going to Tombstone?" Not expecting an answer, Clint looked in the direction that was the subject of all that waving and nodded. "I suppose we are. Come to think of it, we should get there tomorrow."

"Tomorrow," she confirmed.

They finished their supper with a surprising amount of talking. Although they each took turns speaking in their own language, neither one seemed to catch more than a few words from the other. Every so often, Clint would see a glimmer of recognition when he said something to her. He had more success when he approached the conversation using words that anyone might pick up if they spent time around a bunch of folks who all spoke English.

After listening to her as best as he could, Clint swore he heard a few words that sounded vaguely familiar. They could have been bits and pieces he might have picked up while spending time with Chinese or Japanese folks, but they still weren't quite the same. Her language was choppier and somehow more forceful than those other two. It was a piss-poor way to describe it, but it was the best Clint could do after such a long day.

Finally, he stretched out upon the ground and said, "Good night, Lylah."

The fire crackled and a few coyotes howled in the distance. Soon, those noises were joined by the scrape of knees upon the rocky ground. Clint felt a tug upon his shirt. When he turned toward her, she pulled him toward the bedroll that he'd left for her. She crawled around, lay on one half of the bedroll, and motioned for him to come closer.

Clint approached the bedroll and lay down beside her. The firelight brushed over her face just enough for him to see her weary, beautiful smile. "Good night, Clint," she said.

No waving required.

TWENTY

Now that they both knew where they were headed, Clint and Lylah covered a hell of a lot more ground. That was certainly due to Eclipse's natural speed, but it was also because Clint could see a light at the end of the tunnel. Riding for any distance to get to a specific place always seemed better than simply riding without knowing when he could stop. Lylah seemed to prefer it that way, too, since she held on to him and was content to pass the day without so much as one worried gesture to distract him.

They arrived in Tombstone before the sun could dip too close to the western horizon. Clint knew a few shortcuts that got them there a bit quicker than if they'd stuck to the main trail. Also, that allowed him to gain high ground every so often and get a look at the trail he'd left behind. If anyone was following them, they were real good at their job because he didn't pick out one reason to be worried about a tail. Lylah, on the other hand, wasn't so happy to see the Tombstone city limits.

Just to be certain, Clint looked back at her and asked, "Here? Madeline is here?"

Lylah nodded and pointed toward the bustling town as if afraid it might catch her doing so. Grudgingly, she whispered a few words to him and wrapped her arms tightly around his midsection.

At first, Clint thought she was saying something in her own language. Lylah's accent was thick enough to make the few English words she knew a bit difficult to understand. In the short amount of time he'd spent with her, Clint had gotten fairly good at sifting through her accent to find whatever words he could make any sense of. After mulling over the words a few times in his head, Clint asked, "Did you say Hop Town?"

"Hop Town. Yes."

While Clint had been to Tombstone plenty of times, he rarely had occasion to visit the Chinese settlement known to locals as Hop Town. He might have strolled through that area on his way to somewhere else or to see about getting some good food, but most of his business was conducted in Tombstone's saloons or with any number of friends who might be in town while he was there. Having already paid his respects the last time he was in town, Clint avoided his usual haunts and rode down Third Street.

Keeping his head down as he passed Fremont and Allen streets, Clint felt like he was ducking the law or on the run from somebody. The simple fact of the matter was that he didn't know what to expect when dealing with Madeline's situation. He didn't even know what her situation was, but he did know she wasn't too popular with a few lawmen. While he doubted that she had many enemies outside of her own town, Clint didn't want to risk complicating things at this stage of the game.

Then there were all the possibilities that came along with Lylah. Clint had only just started talking to her on a basic level, which meant there was a whole lot of information that was left to his imagination. For all he knew, she was in some sort of trouble. Perhaps she'd been taken under Maddy's wing after running afoul of the law. Maybe that was why she didn't seem too keen on being in Tombstone now.

Perhaps, perhaps, and perhaps some more. The longer Clint thought about all the different ifs and maybes, the more his head ached. It was just easier to keep his hat pulled down, keep his head hung low, and stay out of everyone's notice. In a town like Tombstone, there was never any shortage of distractions.

The closer Clint got to Toughnut Street, the tighter Lylah's arms cinched in around him. When he finally got close enough to see the signs on the buildings change from English to Chinese, he had to fight to draw a breath.

"Easy," he said while patting the little hands that were locked across his stomach. "Where to now?"

Lylah leaned over to get a look at something, but didn't let go of Clint. When she pointed to a stretch of storefronts on the right side of the street, she nearly fell from the saddle and took Clint right along with her. "Madeline . . . in there," she said.

Hearing Lylah form a mostly complete sentence made Clint wonder if she'd been pretending to understand less than she truly did. "Madeline's in there?" he asked, while pointing to a place that looked like a butcher shop.

She shook her head and pointed repeatedly at the store next to the butcher. "Madeline in there!"

"All right, all right. I understand." Lowering his voice, Clint took her hand and eased it down. "No need to tell everyone why we're here."

Lylah looked at him with a mix of confusion and anxiousness on her face. Clint answered that by touching the side of his finger to his lips. That gesture proved to stretch across more than one language, since she nodded and quieted down.

After riding over to the butcher shop, Clint and Lylah dismounted so he could tie the stallion to the closest hitching post. He tipped his hat to a few locals, who barely acknowledged him with a nod. The people who passed him on the street didn't seem rude, but they were all Chinese.

Because of that, they were probably accustomed to much ruder greetings from visitors.

Clint spotted a white man in a rumpled suit staggering from the door of the storefront that Lylah had indicated. Judging by the man's stagger and the cloudiness in his eyes, he was either under the influence of something or had gotten a knock to the head while he was inside. Whichever it was didn't strike Clint as very promising. Looking down at Lylah, he asked, "You sure about this? Madeline is in there?"

She nodded vehemently, pointed at the storefront, and kept her mouth shut.

Clint and Lylah walked past the butcher shop and to the door of the store beside it. There was a large window next to the front door, but it was covered by a thick, dark red curtain. The scent of opium hung in the air and trickled out from under the door. When Clint opened that door, he was nearly dropped by a larger dose of the smoke that washed directly over his face.

This wasn't the sort of place where Clint would expect Madeline to be, but he wasn't about to turn around after riding all this way. If he'd trusted Lylah's directions to bring him this far, he might as well follow them a few more steps. After he took those steps, the door to the opium den slammed shut behind him.

TWENTY-ONE

When the door banged against its frame, none of the people inside the single room took much notice. The Chinese workers who tended to the customers and handed out the pipes were used to the clatter. As for the customers themselves, they probably wouldn't have noticed if the entire building caught fire.

Only one of the three workers approached the front door. The other two were making their rounds among the bunks, cots, and chairs scattered throughout the room. All three were dressed in bright red silk shirts and had towels draped over both shoulders. The worker who came to greet Clint was a woman with a round face, long hair tied into a braid, and a wide, friendly smile.

"I can help you?" she asked.

Clint felt as if he were bowing, simply because he had to bend down so far to talk to the little woman without shouting. "I'm looking for someone and was told she might be here."

"I'm sure we have someone here for you to like," the old woman assured him.

"No, not that kind of someone."

Before Clint could say any more, he noticed that the Chinese woman was no longer looking at him. Her mouth hung open and her eyes grew wide as she finally acknowledged the woman that Clint had brought with him. Until then, Lylah had been treated as just another companion that a customer had bought and paid for as company for when he started puffing from his pipe.

The Chinese woman spoke in her native tongue, but in a slower, more deliberate manner that reminded Clint of the way he spoke to Lylah. This time, however, there was no huffing or eye rolling on Lylah's behalf. She merely smiled and nodded while answering in a few choppy syllables that Clint knew was a simple Chinese greeting.

"Why did you bring her here?" the Chinese woman asked.

Clint had been smiling at the two women's reunion, but that grin faded when he saw the intensity in the Chinese lady's eyes. "It's like I told you before. We're looking for someone."

The Chinese woman grabbed both Clint's and Lylah's arms so she could drag the two farther into the opium den like they were children to be punished. "There are men looking for *her*. Didn't you know that?"

"How was I to know?" Clint asked. "She barely speaks any English. You were talking to her. Maybe you could translate so I can get some more out of her."

"I can hardly say hello and good-bye to her. She knows Chinese as much as she knows English. I can tell you not to be here, though. The men who brought her here want her back. They come looking every day! If they know she here, they will burn my place down. That will start a war."

"Wait. A war? Did I hear you right?"

Gritting her teeth, the Chinese woman dragged Clint and Lylah all the way to the back corner of the room. There was a tapestry hanging from the wall, which Clint thought was probably covering another window. When she pulled it aside, the Chinese woman revealed a narrow door. She unlocked it with a key that hung from a chain around her neck and shoved the other two inside.

"You hear me just fine," the Chinese woman said. "I say war and that's what I mean."

"War with who?" Clint asked.

By this time, Lylah stepped in between the other two as if she were breaking up a fight. Placing one hand upon Clint's chest, she said, "Clint Adams." Touching the Chinese woman's shoulder, she looked at Clint and said, "Ah Chum."

Although those two words sounded like more gibberish, Clint made a guess and asked, "Is that your name? Ah Chum?"

The Chinese woman nodded. "People here call me China Mary."

Now that name did strike a chord with Clint. "China Mary? I've heard of you. I've heard that you call the shots around this part of town."

Mary nodded sagely. The room was a small office. Although it only had enough space for a little rolltop desk, two chairs, and several piles of papers, she settled into her seat as if she were perched upon a throne. "I keep whores in line and opium dens running. Many men work for me and they want to start a war with the men who ride into town with their prisoners and slaves."

"What prisoners and slaves?" Clint asked.

"You look tired," Mary said. "I get you drink? Smoke?"

"No, thanks."

"Then sit. Please."

Since he was too anxious to relax, Clint offered the only other chair to Lylah. It seemed she was just as anxious, because she refused the seat with a quick shake of her head.

Mary may have seemed gentle at first, but that was clearly an act. Now that he'd spent more than a few seconds in her presence, Clint could detect a hardness in her eyes and features that made her face seem more like a visage that had been carefully carved to put folks off their guard. She took a cigar from the box she'd offered to Clint and took her time lighting it. He got the distinct impression that it wouldn't have done one bit of good to try and hurry her.

"I think I hear talk about you, Clint Adams," Mary said as the tip of her cigar flared up. "I hear things from lawmen and hired guns as well. All kinds of things."

"I bet you do. Tell me what you've heard about prisoners and slaves."

Nodding toward Lylah, she muttered, "Why you not ask her?"

"Because she wouldn't understand. I'm asking you now, so why don't you tell me."

Leaning forward with one elbow propped against her knee, Mary waved her cigar at Clint until it got close enough for him to feel the heat from its tip. "You don't tell me what to do. I can call in enough men to cut the Gunsmith down to size before you get to that fancy gun of yours!"

Surprised by the fire in the older woman's eyes, Clint held up his hands to assure her they were nowhere near his holster. "No offense meant."

She looked Clint up and down as if she were fitting him for a coffin. "Maybe you hear of a man named Kyle Morrow."

"Maybe I have."

"Then you know he kidnap women and sell them off after robbing from their men. He also works with slavers who bring girls like that one there into this country."

Clint looked over to Lylah and saw the sorrowful look in her eyes. Even if she didn't know all that was being said, she'd obviously caught enough to get the gist of the conversation.

"You're expecting trouble from Kyle Morrow?" Clint asked.

"I been getting trouble from him for months. It get worse when his merchandise disappear without being paid for. That one there," she added while waving at Lylah, "she run away after I refuse to buy her, so Morrow think I stole her to work in one of my whorehouse. Since then, nothing but trouble from him."

"How did she get away?"

"Help from white lady."

"Madeline Gentry?" Clint asked.

Mary nodded. When she spoke again, there was no longer the edge in her voice that had been there a few moments ago. "Maddy help a lot of girls get away from here. Usually, she take them after they been here for a while so people think they run away on their own. This time, she took that one while Morrow was still in town. Too soon."

"Her name's Lylah."

"What?" Mary snapped.

"That one there. Her name's Lylah."

"They all have name, Mister Adams. I don't remember them until they've been here long enough. That one was supposed to work for me, but she only eat my food, drink my water, and hide in my place of business. I was glad to be rid of her, but you bring her back."

"Funny. You two seemed happy to see each other at first."

Mary flinched as if she'd been caught in a bluff. After a heavy sigh, she slipped right back into her prickly demeanor. "I hoped she could get away before she was killed. I thought she would know to stay away."

"Maddy is the one in trouble. Is she still here?"

"Yes."

"Do you know where I can find her?" Clint asked.

Grudgingly, Mary got up and worked the lock on the door. "Probably best if I take you to her."

TWENTY-TWO

Clint stood in the cemetery, looking down at the unmarked pile of freshly turned soil, and still couldn't believe what he was seeing. Actually, he didn't want to believe the sight in front of him. Lylah had started crying the moment she realized where Mary was taking them. Clint had waited until the last possible moment, hoping that he might find Maddy huddled in a shack somewhere on the property.

"What happened?" he asked.

Still working on the last bit of her cigar, Mary replied, "Kyle Morrow. He killed her, along with some of my people, when he couldn't find that one over there and a few others. My people didn't know where that one went, but Maddy knew. Still, she no say anything."

When he tried to get a read on Mary, Clint came up empty. Sometimes the other woman spoke about Maddy as if she was an enemy, and other times she seemed to truly miss her. Looking down upon the grave, however, Clint had to admit it was too late to worry over what Mary thought about the subject.

From what Clint had heard about China Mary, damn near anything was possible. Just about everyone in Tombstone knew that she was the one to talk to if you had to satisfy any need in Hop Town. Mary ran the whores, the gambling, and the drug trade in that part of town. If you needed anything else after walking past Third and Toughnut streets, Mary could get it for you.

Opinions differed on how Mary ran her businesses. Some said she was as hard as she needed to be, while others called her a small-time dictator. Like anyone else who worked in those kinds of trades, she had gunmen and leg breakers on her payroll right along with the working girls and attendants at her opium den. Some said those gunmen were merely for protection, while others claimed that China Mary had ordered the deaths of anyone who stood in her way.

Having been on the receiving end of plenty of nasty rumors, Clint knew to take them all with a grain of salt. Looking into Mary's eyes and hearing the razor edge in her voice, Clint found it easy to see where some of the nastier rumors about the little woman had come from.

"How'd she die?" Clint asked.

Mary looked at him with one subtly raised eyebrow.

Tired of going back and forth with the Chinese woman, Clint snapped, "Tell me!"

"Kyle Morrow killed her. That's all you need to know. That's all you *want* to know."

"When did this happen?"

"The night after that one—" Seeing the fire in Clint's eyes, Mary started again. "The night after Lylah disappear. He came looking for her, but I didn't know what to tell him. Madeline was there as well. She came to help Lylah and some of the others. I. . . I let some of the youngest ones go with her." When saying that last part, Mary sounded as if she were confessing a sin.

"I get enough girls that work for me who want to be there," Mary continued. "Sometimes, I pay to bring them on. But I don't need slaves. That's messy business. Too messy. But I used to be like some of these younger ones. If I get the chance, I let them go with Maddy. There's not much else I can do for them. If they come back to me, though, it's not good. Make me look bad!"

So it seemed Maddy hadn't been a pariah in just her own town. It was also clear she wasn't the only one in Tombstone. "Are there any others still here?"

"What others?"

"Others like her," he said while pointing at Lylah. "Others who need somewhere else to go."

Mary shook her head. "Maddy had been here not too long ago to get a few. I wasn't expecting her to come again so quick. Lylah was the only one who wanted to go, and it cost Maddy's life. I get enough girls who want to work for me. I pay good and keep them fed. Too risky to use the girls that Kyle Morrow sells."

Considering the law in Tombstone included the Earp brothers, who had occasional help from the likes of Bat Masterson, Mary was dead-on with her assessment. "All right, then," he said. "Where can I find Kyle Morrow?"

Mary turned away from the grave and said, "I don't know and I don't care. The less I know about him, the better."

"I want to find him. What can you do for me?"

"Why do you want to find him?" Mary asked. "Because of what he did to Maddy?"

"Isn't that a good enough reason?"

"Kyle Morrow has done worse, and when he is gone, there will be plenty others to step in and keep doing those same things. Perhaps they think of some new things to do to some new people. Even if half the stories about the Gunsmith are true, you cannot find all the men like Kyle Morrow. Nobody can."

"If I didn't know better, I might think you're trying to keep someone else from being hurt."

Mary grunted something in Chinese that Clint recognized as not too flattering. Then she told him, "I don't know you. I do know Kyle Morrow. I can deal with him or keep him away if I want. If someone else take his place, I have to start all over again."

"What if there is no one to take his place?"

"You really believe that?" she asked with a worldly grin.

Grudgingly, Clint admitted, "Maybe not, but this one will only get worse if he thinks he can get away with killing an innocent woman. There might be a protege, but they should be taught that same lesson by watching what happens to Morrow."

Mary crossed her arms and nodded as if she'd finally decided on what color rug to put in her opium den. "That make sense. I still don't know where to find him, but she does."

Clint looked over to where Mary had nodded and found Lylah silently staring down at Maddy's grave. "Can you help me figure out what she's saying?"

"I don't think I could make her understand your question, but I do know someone who can." She shook her head slowly. "You might want to ask around for someone else, though. Mongolians not as friendly as me."

TWENTY-THREE

Apart from what he'd read in a few ancient history books, Clint wasn't too familiar with Mongolians. He could have met a few here and there while traveling from one spot to another, but he didn't keep track of where they lived or who might be able to translate their language. Since Maddy's killer was probably still not too far away, Clint wanted to act fast before the trail got any colder.

According to Mary, the translator he should talk to lived in a camp up in the Whetstone Mountains. That wasn't more than fifteen or twenty miles away, so he figured he could take a bit of time and do some more asking around Tombstone. He was on good terms with the Earp brothers, but they weren't the law in town any longer. There was one man who might just be a bigger help to Clint than any lawman. If anyone was to know the whereabouts of an outlaw like Kyle Morrow, it was a bounty hunter. And in Cochise County, there weren't many bounty hunters who knew their trade better than Eddie Sanchez.

If he was in Tombstone, Eddie could be found in a rented room on the second floor of a rat trap on Fifth Street. When Clint arrived at the run-down little boardinghouse, he asked the redheaded man behind the front desk if Eddie was available.

"Yeah," the redhead told him as he plastered his eyes onto Lylah. "He's here."

Before the redhead could drool or reach out to grab her, Clint pulled Lylah closer to him and asked, "Which room is he in?"

"Same as always. If you want yer own room, I got one open."

"No, thanks."

As Clint walked toward the stairs, the redhead asked, "You wanna send her my way when you're through?"

Clint stopped and glared at the redhead in a way that made it clear just how far he'd stepped in the wrong direction. Without saying another word, the redhead looked away and found something else to do.

"Don't mind that," Clint said as he took Lylah with him. She might not have understood what he muttered, but he could tell that she knew what the redhead was after without being told.

Eddie's usual room was at the end of the hall on the second floor, overlooking the street. Before Clint could knock upon the door, it was opened. A full-figured woman with stringy brown hair emerged from the room while adjusting her large breasts within her partially buttoned blouse. She smirked at Clint, sneered at Lylah, and headed for the stairs.

"Hello, Eddie," Clint said as he stepped inside.

The bounty hunter was a big man with enough hair on his chest and back to create a natural rug. "That you, Adams? You should'a been here earlier. Missed one hell of a performance."

"From you or the woman who's paid to pretend enjoying being with you?" Clint asked.

"Real damn funny." Standing up without making a move to retrieve his shirt or even adjust his britches so he wasn't exposing himself to everyone within eyeshot, Eddie asked, "Who's that you got with ya?"

"Nobody you need to worry about, so keep it in your pants."

"All right, all right. I comprende."

"You heard me, Eddie. Keep it in your pants."

Smirking as he reached between his legs, Eddie fitted himself back within his trousers and hitched them up a bit. "What brings you to town? You wanna lose some more money to me by betting on a gut-shot straight draw?"

"Nothing like that. I've got a few questions for you. Have you ever heard of Kyle Morrow?"

"The slaver and kidnapper who sells sweet little ladies to everyone in the Arizona Territories?"

"That's the one."

"Never heard of him," Eddie said with a grin that showed a collection of yellowed, crooked teeth that had plenty of gaping holes.

"I want to track him down."

"That might not be a great idea."

"Fine," Clint said. "Then what do you know about a group of Mongolians camped in the Whetstone Mountains?"

"Plenty. I trade with 'em and they cook one hell of a good meal."

"I want to know how to get there. I can pay for the information."

Stepping up close to Clint, Eddie draped an arm over his shoulders and pulled him in close. "What's the matter, Adams? You in a rush? It seems like you don't wanna shoot the breeze unless I can give you whatever information you're after."

"I told you what I'm after and I told you I'd pay for it."

"So you don't wanna be social no more? You sore about them poker losses?"

"No, Eddie." Clint sighed. "This room stinks and you

stink worse. I've got a killer to hunt down and if I stay around here much longer, that letch downstairs will probably slink up here to try and grope under this woman's skirts."

The bounty hunter nodded and looked around as if to verify what Clint had said. He stuck his nose near his own armpit, pulled in a breath, and said, "You make a bunch of valid points. Here's another one for ya. Kyle Morrow is worth a whole lot of money. There are rewards for his scalp placed by half a dozen families that are missing women on account of that prick. I ain't about to just hand him over."

"I thought you didn't know where to find him."

"I said it wouldn't be a good idea to track him down," Eddie corrected. "Not on yer own, anyway. It ain't a good idea for me to go on my own, either, which is why I ain't scalped him myself. I ain't one for partners, but you could fit the bill."

"I didn't come here for a partner," Clint said.

"So you wanna just hunt down a man like Kyle Morrow? That lady you got with ya must be one hell of a wildcat if she's about to back you up against Morrow and his whole gang."

"How big is his gang?"

Eddie knew he was gaining ground, just like a wolf knew when there was easy prey nearby. Grinning like a hungry animal, he said, "Big enough to get the drop on you whether you get to Morrow or not. The two of us could do the job, though. If that lady comes along as an extra set of eyes, she could watch our backs to even out the odds more. All she'd have to do is let out a yell when someone's comin' and we could—"

"You talk a lot," Clint grunted. "If we're to ride together, that's gotta change."

"So we're partners?"

"Do you know where to find Morrow?"

"I got some ideas," Eddie replied. When Clint waved him off and turned to leave, the bounty hunter grabbed his arm and quickly added, "I know how his gang works, where they like to hole up, what towns they like to visit, and which whores they fuck when they visit them."

"You really know all of that?" Clint asked.

Eddie nodded. "I been collecting all I can about Morrow, savin' up for when I was ready to strike out after him. All I been missin' was a few good partners and the location of one of Morrow's camps. Without someplace to start, I'd just be ridin' in circles hoping to cross paths with the son of a bitch."

"You know which haystack, but still need to pick out the needle, huh?"

Snapping his fingers, Eddie said, "You always were real good with words. You're also the only partner I need to go after Morrow and the men he's got with him. Plus," he added with a sly flick of his eyebrows, "the more of 'em we can drag in, the bigger the payday when we're through."

"What else can you tell me about him?"

"Just that he's slippery as an eel and twice as dangerous. That is, the poisonous eels. The dangerous kind. Are eels dangerous?"

"What if I can take you to one of Morrow's camps?" Clint asked. "Would that be enough for you to track him if he's not there when we arrive?"

The smile on the bounty hunter's face might have been filthy, but it was earnest. "If I know what direction they headed from that spot, I could get ahead of them assholes with time to spare."

Clint studied the bounty hunter, ignoring the way he anxiously shifted from one foot to another like a little boy waiting to get a birthday present. Eddie Sanchez wasn't exactly an upstanding citizen, but he was a damn good tracker and could handle himself in a fight. Anyone who enjoyed sleeping with other men's wives as much as Eddie did had to know how to handle himself.

"What about that camp in the mountains?" Clint asked.

"I know a shortcut. We can be there before supper to-morrow. I'm tellin' you, those fellas can cook good enough to make your head—"

"All right, Eddie, we're partners. Just shut up, get some sleep, and take a bath."

Eddie saluted Clint, winked at Lylah, and scratched his crotch.

TWENTY-FOUR

It was a dusty ride to the Whetstone Mountains. The range wasn't one of the most impressive Clint had ever seen, since they rose up from the ground more like a tall set of ridges instead of mountains as majestic as the Rockies. Still, they were a sight to behold as they drew closer. When he motioned for Eddie to stop, Clint kept his eyes on the mountains and looked for anything that might be a camp.

"Where are we headed?" he asked.

Eddie brought his horse to a stop and reached for his canteen. After splashing a good portion of water upon the front of his shirt, he wiped his mouth and grunted, "Ride toward that southern slope. The Baht moves his men around a lot, but the camp more or less stays put."

"Did you say Bat?"

"Bahhht," Lylah said. Until now, she'd been so quiet that Clint had nearly forgotten she was there. Her arms had been locked around him all day and her head was almost always pressed against his shoulder. When Clint turned to look at her, she pulled down the scarf that had been wrapped around her face to keep the dust from her mouth and pronounced the name a little slower.

"All right," Clint replied. "Who is that?"

Lylah didn't have an answer for that, so she nestled in behind him again.

"Baht is the head honcho at that camp," Eddie explained. "I've dealt with him a few times, so let me do the talkin'."

"How about you get us there first?"

"Sure enough. Follow me." With that, Eddie snapped his reins and rode toward the southern portion of the mountain range.

Despite the fact that they could see the mountains plain as day, it took a few more hours before they got close enough to look for the camp. Just when Clint was about to accuse Eddie of leading them in circles, he picked out a trail of smoke that resembled a smudge in the sky leading down to a spot at the base of the mountains. They rode toward that for a little while longer before Clint spotted something else in the distance.

"Is that your friend?" he asked as he pointed to a cluster of four men on horseback a little ways ahead of them.

"There's one way to find out." Eddie tapped his heels against his horse's sides, prompting the animal to break into a gallop.

Clint patted Lylah's hands, which caused her to cinch her arms a bit tighter around his midsection. Since she was squared away, Clint allowed Eclipse to tear after Eddie amid a thunder of hooves. Not long after catching up to the bounty hunter, Clint heard the hiss of something whip between him and Eddie. The crack of a distant rifle soon followed.

"I thought you recognized them!" Clint said.

Eddie pulled hard on his reins and steered his horse sharply off its previous course. "That's Baht, all right," he groaned. "We might have left off on a sour note the last time I was out this way."

Another shot was fired that got close enough to make Clint duck down out of reflex. "Sour enough to shoot us on sight?"

Although the bounty hunter didn't give a straight answer, he squirmed enough to tell Clint what he wanted to know.

"Some partner I got," Clint snarled.

TWENTY-FIVE

More shots hissed through the air above Clint's head and on either side. Either those men were deliberately trying to miss or they all needed spectacles. Gambling on the former, Clint drew his pistol and looked over at Eddie. "Do you trust me?"

The bounty hunter grinned widely and drew his own gun. "We gotta drop every one of these men before they can send word back to their camp, but if anyone can do it, we can!"

Two of the four riders broke off from the group to hang back and watch Clint, Lylah, and Eddie. The remaining two thundered straight ahead as if they fully intended on stampeding directly over all three of the new arrivals.

"You'll do what I say and follow my lead?" Clint asked.

"Hell yes!"

"Good," Clint said as he placed the barrel of his Colt flush against Eddie's forehead. "Now holster your pistol and keep your mouth shut."

The bounty hunter clenched his jaw with enough force to crack his own teeth. Whether it was his faith in Clint or the gun pointed at him, he followed orders to the letter.

Since Eddie seemed to be under control, Clint looked

toward the approaching riders. The two that hung back were sighting down rifles and the first two had slowed to a trot as they drew closer. In addition to that, several other men on horseback appeared on one of the lower ridges of the mountain range. Clint didn't need to use his spyglass to know that they were most likely taking aim at him with rifles of their own.

One of the riders who approached was a young man with dark skin and blunt features. He had a wide nose, narrowed eyes, and a thick mustache hanging from his upper lip like a tattered curtain. When he spoke, it was with an accent that was close enough to Lylah's to let Clint know they'd come to the right place.

"Drop your guns and come with us," the rider said.

"The hell I will," Clint replied. "I dragged this son of a bitch this far and I'm not about to lower my weapon now."

"You had it lowered before. You can lower it again."

"That was before we got here. Are you Baht?"

The rider nodded as he sized up all three people in front of him.

"My name's Clint Adams and I heard you got a bone to pick with this man."

"That's right."

"You willing to pay to get your hands on him?"

Baht smirked and nodded. "We can offer you a few things. If he's a prisoner, why does he carry a weapon?"

"Because he didn't know he was a prisoner until now," Clint replied. "Since there's more than just me and a woman to deal with him now, I can finally turn him over and stop acting like his friend."

"You son of a bitch," Eddie growled. If he was acting, the bounty hunter was doing a fine job, because he looked more than ready to pull Clint's head off.

TWENTY-SIX

Baht switched his pistol to his left hand so he could take a sawed-off shotgun from the boot of his saddle. Not only had the barrel been shortened, but the grip had been replaced with a chunky version of a pistol grip to make it easier to hold without being braced against a shooter's shoulder. Baht handled the awkward weapon well enough to show that he knew how to use it just fine.

"We can offer food, provisions, and perhaps some money for this one," Baht said. "Agreed?"

"There's a favor I need to ask," Clint said. "I need someone to translate."

"Translate?"

"That's right." Pointing at Lylah, Clint said, "She doesn't speak English and I need someone to help translate. I'm told she speaks your language."

Looking at him as if Clint was speaking nonsense, Baht said, "English is my language."

"Then what about someone else in your camp? This woman is Mongolian and—"

"Yes, I can see what she is," Baht snapped. Obviously impatient to shoot Eddie and be done with it, he said, "A few old men in our camp speak the old tongue. They'll be happy to translate once I bring this one's head in a sack."

"Can't let you do that," Clint said.

"Why not?"

"I want to bring him in alive. You wouldn't want to lose what he took from you."

Baht scowled at Eddie and then lowered his shotgun. "No, I suppose not." Staring at the bounty hunter the way a hungry cat might fix upon a dead fish, he said, "Give me his weapon."

"You heard the man, Eddie," Clint said. "Hand it over."

The bounty hunter complied and stayed still as his knife was taken out of the scabbard hanging from his belt and the rifle was taken from the boot of his saddle. The other dark-skinned man who'd ridden with Baht circled around to ride behind Clint and Eddie as Baht led them all toward the mountains.

They found a narrow path winding between some piles of rocks that led up a ridge and down another trail. The Whetstones were just big enough to offer sanctuary from the dusty winds and keep the camp out of plain sight. By the time they arrived at the settlement, Clint saw several men watching them from various lookout points around the camp's perimeter.

The camp was made up of several tents crafted from pelts and furs instead of canvas. Shelters of various sizes, all with rounded tops, were clustered together like a bunch of dirt mounds that had been left behind by some very large prairie dogs. People roamed among the shelters, tending to animals, washing clothes, and preparing food at one of the fires that had sent up the smoke Clint had spotted earlier.

Baht dismounted and walked away, letting one of his men point a gun at Clint and Eddie.

"Off the horses," the man said.

Once all three had dismounted, more men appeared to

take the reins. Eclipse protested immediately, but Clint calmed the Darley Arabian with a few pats on the muzzle.

"How'd you know I took somethin' from these men?" Eddie whispered.

"I figured it was a safe bet, considering how badly they wanted to shoot you. If I was wrong, I could have told them you *did* take something and I'm sure they would have believed me."

As much as Eddie looked like he wanted to defend his character, he couldn't put together a convincing argument. "So you just hand me over to these savages? They can kill me at any time, you know."

"They could have killed all of us when we first arrived," Clint pointed out. "Considering that you didn't mention the reception we might get, I wouldn't mind killing you myself."

Once more, Eddie was unable to come up with a good defense. "I thought you were better than this, Adams. Stabbin' a man in the back ain't your style."

The man who came over to collect Eddie stood a full head taller than the bounty hunter. He was a solid, imposing figure covered in thick layers of muscle that made him as big around as a tree trunk. His glistening white teeth could barely be seen through the thick beard that covered the bottom portion of his face and hung down to well past his neck.

"What did you take from these people, Eddie?" Clint asked. "Tell me quick."

"Some gold trinkets. They looked old."

Clint nodded and stepped back as the big fellow moved in close enough to snarl at him like a wolf claiming a fresh kill. "Take him away but don't harm him," Clint warned.

"Why?" the big fellow asked.

"Because I was promised some things and I want to make sure I get them." Noticing the predatory gleam in the bigger man's eyes, Clint added, "You kill him and you'll never get your gold back."

The big man gnashed his teeth and snarled.

Stepping around the big man while patting him on the shoulder, Baht said, "Take him to sit with the horses, Tumen. I want to have a few words with Mister Sanchez, and he'll need his tongue for that."

Tumen liked the sound of that, so he grabbed Eddie by the scruff of his neck and shoved him farther into the camp.

"Come with me," Baht said. "There is someone you might like to meet."

TWENTY-SEVEN

Some of the larger structures at the center of the camp were set up with rough wooden frames. Once he was inside one of them, Clint could see the frames were actually put together in complex patterns that supported the animal skin shell over the space that might be occupied by a small cabin. There was a small cot within the shelter, along with a few chairs and a table that looked as if it had fallen off the back of a wagon while on its way to a rich man's sitting room.

Baht motioned toward the shelter's only other occupant, who was a short, solidly built man with scraggly gray hair that was gathered at the back of his head and held in place with a leather thong. "This is Chuluun," Baht said. "He grew up in the old country and knows the old tongue."

"You know the old tongue just as I do," Chuluun scolded. "At least, you would know it if you had listened when I tried to teach you." Before Baht could say anything, the old man stuck a finger out at him and said, "Many times, I tried to teach you! You never listen." Looking at Clint, he added, "He never listens."

Clint shrugged. "Kids."

"Yes. Yes, indeed. So," the old man said as he studied Clint's face, "who are you?"

"This is Clint Adams," Baht replied. "He brought back the bounty hunter who stole our coins."

"Are the coins here?" Chuluun asked.

"He says he wants a favor first."

"Nobody does kind things for free anymore," the old man sighed. "Then again, I suppose it is just as well, since we stole those coins in the first place."

"Took them from a grave-robbing Army caravan!" Baht corrected. "Those are ours by right!"

Chuluun waved at the younger man as if he was growing more tired of the conversation by the second. "Everything comes around. What's the favor you want, Clint Adams?"

Clint reached back until he felt his hand bump against the woman who had been all but forgotten by the rugged, dark-skinned men who lived in the camp. "This," he said, "is Lylah. At least, that's the name she was given by the woman who used to be taking care of her."

Examining her the way he might examine a horse, Chuluun asked, "She is your favor?"

"Kind of. I'm told that she's Mongolian. I was also told that you might be able to help translate for me so we could ask her a few questions."

"What kind of questions?"

"There's a man we're after," Clint replied. "A killer. He killed the woman who used to care for Lylah and he's killed several others. He's also a kidnapper and a slave trader."

"So many evils wrapped up into one person," Chuluun said. "Are you sure this isn't a monster that comes in the night?"

Picking up on the old man's chuckle and the smirk upon his face, Clint said, "This man's real enough. His name is Kyle Morrow."

Chuluun's smile dried up right away. "I have heard of him."

"Me, too," Baht said. "If I knew where he was, I would have killed him myself."

Since Lylah had nestled in close to him, Clint draped a protective arm around her as he said, "Well, she does know where he is. I just can't understand what she's saying."

"Then how do you know what she knows?" Chuluun asked.

Trying not to sound as frustrated as he felt, Clint replied, "She's been to Morrow's camp. If we can get back there, I could track him down. She might have other information as well. Perhaps she knows where Morrow was headed. Maybe she heard him say something. There could be any number of things to help us find this bastard."

Chuluun nodded. "You were close to this woman who was killed."

"Yes, but there were children involved."

"Kyle Morrow killed her children?" Baht asked.

Clint let out a measured breath and said, "They were children who traveled with her when she was hurt. Or maybe they weren't with her at the time. I don't know, and that's what's killing me. It's bad enough that she's dead. She was a good woman who only wanted to help folks and she caught nothing but grief for it. Morrow has to answer for her, but if he did hurt those children . . ."

"Then he should be cut open and left for the rats," Chuluun said in a steely tone. "And what of the bounty hunter? Did you bring him this far to help you track Kyle Morrow?"

"We're not letting him go," Baht said.

Chuluun silenced him with a simple glance. "We will discuss the bounty hunter later," he said to both Clint and Baht. "Let's see if this girl and I can have a chat."

TWENTY-EIGHT

The shelter where Eddie was kept wasn't as wide as a small bedroom and was too short for anyone inside to stand up straight. Since Eddie had his hands tied behind his back to a post and his legs stretched out in front of him, he didn't have to worry about standing up. The skins forming the walls of the shelter were thick enough to keep out the outside light, but a trickle of it came in from the bottom edge for him to watch as the daylight faded into night.

He struggled until his wrists bled, but to no avail. The ropes were strong. The knots were tight and the post was sunk down far enough into the ground to keep from budging. Eddie could hear movement outside the shelter, but couldn't make any sounds of his own thanks to the cloth that had been wadded up and stuffed into his mouth.

When the flap at the front of the shelter was pulled aside, Eddie straightened up with his back against the post. His knees came up toward his chest in preparation to kick whatever target presented itself. Oddly enough, the woman who hurried into the shelter smiled warmly at him as she removed the cloth from his mouth. She was a slender woman, who was almost as tall as any of the men in the camp. She had the wide, rounded features of the others, but had somewhat lighter skin, and eyes that sparkled as if they'd seen just a bit more than she would ever let on.

Crouching down upon one knee put her at Eddie's level while also exposing one long, muscular leg through a slit in her buckskin dress. Normally, the slit would have simply allowed her to walk and ride a horse a bit easier, but she'd hiked the skirt up a little so she could hunker down in front of the bounty hunter.

"What the hell, Nayan?" Eddie hissed after spitting out the cloth. "It's only been a week."

"You weren't supposed to come back at all, Eddie."

"But you said Baht wouldn't even notice those coins were missing for at least another month. You swore nobody even looked at them more than a few times a year."

Nayan shrugged and told him, "One of those times was a few days ago. Our agreement was that you would take the blame for stealing the coins whenever they came up missing. Why did you come back here?"

"I thought I had more time before Baht wanted to kill me. And," he added with a sheepish grin, "I missed seein' your pretty face."

Although Nayan didn't stop smiling, she shifted it into something much more sinister than it had been when she'd first discovered him. "I'm not stupid, Eddie. Tell me why you're really here. Is it something to do with that woman and the other white man?"

"Those two are gonna help me find Kyle Morrow. Him and anyone he's ridden with for more than a day or two are worth a fortune."

"How are you going to spend that much money if your head is stuck upon a post outside this camp?"

"That's . . . uhhh . . . where I figured you might come in."

She nodded and sighed, "I thought so."

"Get me out of here and I'll cut you in on the reward money I get for Morrow."

"Him and his partners?"

Wincing as if he'd been jabbed below the belt, Eddie said, "All right. Ten percent of my share."

"Fifty."

"What?" He winced again as he looked toward the door. When nobody responded to his raised voice right away, he dropped it to an urgent whisper and asked, "Fifty percent?"

"Your partner seems to have left you here to rot," she pointed out. "Without me, you won't get anything but a blade across your throat."

"You'd let me die for what we did? And my partner hasn't forgotten about me. He's got his business to conduct, but he stopped Baht from killing me outright. I bet he's negotiating my release right now."

"You sure about that?" she asked.

"Yeah. And if I recall, stealing them coins was your idea."

"A lot of folks get a lot of ideas, but the ones who see those ideas through are the ones who've got to pay for them." After letting him stew on that for a few seconds, Nayan leaned in close enough to whisper into his ear. "If you've still got those coins, we can put them back and put this whole thing behind us. I'll convince Baht that they were just misplaced."

"I . . . uhhh . . . already sold 'em."

"And what about my cut of that money?" When she saw that no answer was forthcoming, she patted his cheek and said, "Didn't think so."

"I told you I'd have your cut when we met up again in the fall, and I'll have it."

"I know, Eddie."

"So, you'll let me out?"

"As long as you have my fifty percent of that reward money on top of what you owe me for the coins."

"The coin money plus your thirty percent will be there when we meet in the fall."

"Forty percent, or you stay right here and wait for your

partner to arrive. Just hope his negotiations are done before Baht gets too impatient."

"You've got a deal," Eddie said. "Now get me out of here."

Nayan allowed her grin to lose some of its edge as she pulled up her skirts and climbed onto him so she could straddle his lap while facing him.

"What the hell are you doing?" Eddie asked.

"Seeing you tied up like this is kind of nice," she purred. "I like knowing you can't get away from me."

"You wanna get close? We can do it later. Just . . ." Eddie's words were cut short when he felt her tug at his belt and unfasten his pants.

As she worked to pull his pants down, Nayan never looked away from Eddie's face. She stared straight into his eyes and raised her eyebrows when her hands finally reached what they'd been seeking. "Seems like you missed this just as much as I did."

Eddie squirmed, but didn't want to move too much. She was stroking his cock up and down, working his erection into something that was hard enough to ache. "Jesus, girl," he snarled. "You never wanna do this in a bed. Always when we shouldn't even think about it."

"I'm always thinking about it," she replied as she lifted herself up enough to gather her skirts around her waist. Beneath her dress she wore simple undergarments that were easily pulled aside so she could fit him between her legs as she settled back down on him.

Her pussy was wet and warm as it wrapped around his rigid penis and eased all he way down to the base. Nayan sat facing him and slowly ground her hips while placing her hands upon his shoulders.

"Someone's gonna . . . gonna check on me . . . before too long," Eddie said as she rocked slowly on top of him.

"Then we'd better be quick."

"Ain't there a . . . better time for this?"

"You want me to stop?" she asked.

"No . . . I just . . ." Eddie pulled even harder at the ropes that bound his hands but still couldn't get them free. He could move his legs, however, so he dug his heels into the dirt to give him some purchase as he pumped his cock up into her.

Nayan responded to that with a breathy sigh and locked her fingers behind his neck as she rode him harder. "How could any bed compare to this?" she whispered. "Isn't this exciting? Doesn't it make you feel alive?"

"That's what you said when we stole them coins," Eddie pointed out.

Just mentioning the theft made Nayan grab him tighter. Eddie swore he felt her pussy grow a little wetter as it cinched in around him. All he had to do was pump into her harder as he continued talking.

"You wanna fuck when I'm about to get killed?" he snarled. "I can't think of a better way to go. Too bad I can't bend you over something and fuck you from behind like I did the night we stole that gold. You liked that, didn't you?"

"Oh yes," Nayan whispered as she bounced faster in his lap.

"You like being bad?"

"Yes."

"You're a bad little whore, ain't you?"

Nayan's fingernails dug into his neck and a tremor worked its way through her lower body. "Yes!"

Eddie barely even realized how loud she'd been. Nayan had built up a good rhythm and was sliding up and down the entire length of his erection. Just a few more bounces and he would . . .

"What is this?" one of the men from the camp bellowed as he stomped into the shelter.

Nayan stood up and quickly pulled her dress down to cover herself.

"Is he loose?"

"No," she replied. "I thought his ropes had come untied, so I tightened them."

"Why did you scream?" the man asked.

"Just calling for someone to help me. Glad you were so quick." Nayan gave Eddie an apologetic shrug before stepping aside.

"She was doing just fine," Eddie whined. "Couldn't you just give her another minute?"

TWENTY-NINE

Chuluun and Lylah spoke for hours. Although Clint couldn't understand what they were saying, their gestures and her facial expressions told him that they spent the first bit of time with simple questions so the old man could gain her trust. When Lylah's eyes narrowed into a steely gaze and her voice was strained to the point of breaking, Clint figured she was talking about her time with Kyle Morrow. Whenever the outlaw's name was mentioned, she toughened up a little more.

Some food was brought in for everyone, which consisted of strips of meat in a spicy sauce. As they ate, the talking continued. Every so often, Clint spotted tears at the corners of Lylah's eyes. Just when he was about to step in and insist on taking a rest for a few minutes, she wiped her face dry and soldiered on.

A woman cried out from somewhere else in the camp, which Clint thought was peculiar. He thought she sounded like she was in the throes of passion, but that couldn't have been right. Judging by the commotion that followed the woman's yell, she probably had an accident or was signaling one of the men guarding the camp's perimeter. Before

Clint could get too involved with that, Chuluun stood up and walked over to him.

"Well, I believe I know her language," the old man said.

"I kind of guessed that. What did she say?"

"She has endured much since coming to this country, which was less than a year ago. Since then, she has been a slave, escaped captivity, was captured, escaped again, and then was kidnapped by Kyle Morrow," Chuluun explained. "It was simple luck that your friend Madeline managed to find her when she did. From what I was told, Lylah slipped away just long enough for Madeline to find her. Somehow Madeline knew she was in trouble and took Lylah under her wing."

Clint nodded. "Sounds about right."

"Kyle Morrow tracked down Lylah in Tombstone, but Madeline bought enough time for her to get away. The last time Lylah saw her, Madeline was about to try to send Morrow and his men in the wrong direction."

"What about the children?" Clint asked. "Did she mention anything about children being with Madeline?"

"No, but I can ask." Chuluun turned toward Lylah, who sat cross-legged and hunched over a plate of food. After trading a few quick lines in their native language, the old man turned toward Clint and said, "She heard Madeline talk about two children, but didn't see them herself."

"That means they could be with Morrow. Damn."

There was another possibility, but Clint didn't want to think about that. He was riled up enough already.

"She was at Morrow's home," Chuluun said.

"She knows where he's camped?"

"She knows where he lives. It sounds like he has deep roots in a town somewhere near Prescott."

"Can she get us there?" Clint asked hopefully.

The old man nodded. "I can talk with her and draw a map. Would that be good?"

"That would be great."

"Excellent. Before I do that, there is something I need from you." As Chuluun said that, Baht walked up to stand closer to Clint. "The bounty hunter you brought in took something that belonged to our entire tribe. Since you brought him here, I am guessing you already know about this."

"I heard that Eddie made off with something, but I don't know what it was," Clint replied, sticking as close to the truth as possible. So far, that hadn't been much of a problem.

"So, you brought him here to trade for my help with your situation?" Chuluun asked.

Clint was always amazed at how much his poker experience translated into life away from the game. Right now he could tell that the old man knew a lot more than he was saying. Every instinct in Clint's head told him to not even bother trying to bluff someone with such clear, intense eyes.

Cutting straight to the quick, Chuluun asked, "You didn't know he was wanted by our people, did you?"

"No, sir. He offered to bring me here so you could translate."

"He . . . came here on his own accord?"

"More or less," Clint replied.

"And why did you hand him over to us?"

"Your men were anxious to get to him and they were itching for a fight," Clint said. "Before any blood was spilt, I gave them what they wanted and tried to make sure Eddie wasn't hurt. Well . . . not hurt too badly, at least."

Chuluun's eyes narrowed further as he studied Clint.

"Send this traitor away," Baht said. "We have the thieving bounty hunter and he has his translation. He can leave the woman behind as well."

"Shut your mouth, boy!" Chuluun roared.

Baht backed down so fast that he reflexively took a step toward the door. Regaining his composure, he straightened and puffed out his chest. He did not, however, step forward to where he'd been a few seconds ago.

In a level voice, Chuluun said, "Baht, shoot Mister Adams."

The younger man grinned and reached for the gun holstered at his side. He barely slipped his finger beneath the trigger guard before Clint drew his Colt and took aim in a single, fluid motion.

Stepping forward to stand between the other two men, Chuluun said, "I believe Mister Adams spoke the truth. If he'd wanted to fight, there would have been a fight. From what I've just seen, it would have been a most impressive fight. Where is the bounty hunter?"

"Tumen says Nayan was with the thief. She is the one who called out."

Chuluun rolled his eyes. "That woman . . . Are you sure she does not have the coins?"

"I told you already. We searched her belongings twice."

"Search them again and bring the bounty hunter here."

"What about Nayan?" Baht asked.

"I don't want to hear her speak another word," the old man said in a disgusted tone. "Most of her words are too hollow to bear any weight."

THIRTY

Clint and Lylah were left alone in Chuluun's shelter, but it was obvious that they weren't meant to leave. Men were posted just outside the hut and several more scurried throughout the camp just beyond Clint's sight. After the better part of an hour had gone by, Clint was feeling restless.

"They say they want to get their hands on Eddie, but why do I feel like the prisoner here?" he muttered.

Lylah looked at him, but didn't respond.

Clint's hand drifted toward his pistol. He knew he could make it out of the hut and probably to Eclipse, but wasn't certain just how much dust would be kicked up in the process. He'd gotten a good look at the camp and had a vague idea of how many men he'd have to face. Even so, he wasn't sure if facing them was a good idea. He'd survived plenty of scrapes by listening to his instincts and following his gut, but every so often those same things got him into trouble. At the moment, it was difficult to figure out which category this situation fell into.

Just as Clint was about to test the waters of leaving the hut, the men outside stepped away from the door to allow Chuluun to return. The old man held several things collected in his arms, none of which seemed very threatening.

"I brought some things for Lylah," Chuluun said. "She can draw a map and any instructions you might need. I will write the words as well as some notes from when we were speaking, since I am not about to go with you on your ride."

"Can you tell her that she doesn't have to go?" Clint requested. "I don't want her to be put into any more danger than necessary."

"Oh, I already told her that. I offered her a place here for a while and even gave her a chance to tell us if she was being held captive or mistreated. You'll be happy to know she had nothing but kind words to say about you."

"Yeah," Clint said as he watched Tumen step into the hut and glare at him, "that is good to know. Tell me something, Chuluun. Is that her real name? I think it was given to her by Madeline, but she must have a proper name."

"She does."

"You already asked her that?"

"We spoke for a long time," Chuluun said. "She is a friendly woman and very pretty. I am a man, so I enjoy speaking with friendly, pretty women. I asked about her birth name, but she did not want to tell me. It seems she has great affection for Madeline and, out of respect for her, wishes to keep the name she's been given."

Clint looked at Lylah, who'd taken an interest in the conversation since Maddy's name had been mentioned. Nodding solemnly, Lylah smiled at Clint and got to work drawing upon the parchment that Chuluun had given her.

"You should know that it is because of what she said that you and your partner are to be set free," Chuluun added.

"Is that so?"

"Indeed. Coming here with that bounty hunter was a risky move, but I believe that you were not aware of this risk. As for the bounty hunter, well, there's only one way for us to know what he might have been thinking."

As if on cue, Eddie was shoved into the hut. He knocked

against Tumen like he'd hit a brick wall. To his credit, Eddie looked as if he meant to scold that wall for being built in such an inconvenient place.

"What brings you here, Eddie?" Clint asked before the bounty hunter could say anything he might instantly regret.

"A few assholes who smell like wet dog brought me here," Eddie replied.

Tumen grabbed the bounty hunter by the front of his shirt and pulled him to stand beside Clint.

"The only reason you're not dead," Chuluun said to Eddie, "is because of Nayan's history of stealing from her own people. She says you stole our gold and I'm sure you will point the finger back at her. What I want to know is why you came back to this camp at all."

Clint watched the bounty hunter, wishing he could just tell the other man what to say. Before he could attempt any prompting, Eddie spoke on his own behalf.

"I came back because Clint needed help and you're the only ones who could do the job."

"And you gave no thought to the missing coins?" Chuluun asked.

Eddie shrugged and said, "I honestly didn't think they'd be missed yet."

It was a truth given because there was nothing left to lose. Clint recognized the tired resignation that seeped into Eddie's voice like cold water through a leaky roof. The old man must have noticed it as well, because he accepted it almost immediately.

"Mister Adams has gotten the help he wanted," Chuluun said. He then raised a finger and added, "But we will get our property back as well. Since I have heard too many bad things about Kyle Morrow, I will allow all three of you to go after him."

Eddie let out a relieved sigh and even chuckled a bit when he said, "You've made the right choice. As soon as this is done, I'll bring back them coins."

"I know you will," the old man said. "Because I'm sending someone with you to make sure of it."

Baht stepped up and declared, "I will make sure the job is done properly or I'll bring the bounty hunter's head back on a stake."

The old man shook his head. "No, you won't. You have spent too many nights with Nayan. That's why Tumen will go with them."

Baht sputtered a bit, but didn't even try to change the old man's mind. Tumen crossed his arms and stood there like a carving chipped from stone.

"And if he doesn't return with the coins," Chuluun added, "our people will not rest until both of the white men's heads are on stakes. The woman is not to be harmed, Tumen. She's seen enough pain."

THIRTY-ONE

The next morning, Clint and Lylah rode out on Eclipse while Eddie and Tumen rode with them on their own horses. Lylah had been offered the use of a horse, but she insisted on staying with Clint. The truth of the matter was that Clint was getting used to her being back there as well. If she was coming along, it just wouldn't have felt right to not feel her arms wrapped around his midsection or her head resting upon the back of his shoulder.

But that's not to say the ride was a quiet one.

"I hope you're happy, Clint," Eddie groused. "You pull that gun on me, get me tossed into something close to a jail, nearly get me executed, and then allow this beast to tag along with us."

"You're the one who brought us here," Clint reminded him.

"But you didn't have to serve me up like that!"

"I wasn't going to let them kill you."

"Really? And how were you gonna stop them? I suppose you had a rescue all planned out?"

"I spoke to Chuluun and some of the others. Besides, you did steal from them. You could've told me we might be walking into a camp full of angry armed men."

"If you must know," Eddie said, "I wanted to get us close enough for you to ride in so I could stay behind and meet up with you when you were finished."

Clint nodded and watched the trail ahead. "Ahhh. So that was your plan, huh?"

"It sure was. If I would'a known you'd stick a gun in my face and let me get tossed into a stinking pit like an animal, I wouldn't have even agreed to help you."

Tumen's laugh was so low and so gravelly that it almost blended perfectly with the crunch of the horses' hooves against the ground. When Clint looked over at the big man, he was surprised to see a wide smile covering Tumen's face.

"Yeah," Eddie sneered. "Laugh it up. Step too far out of line and I'll knock you off that horse. I don't give a damn how many Mongolians might come after us. Let 'em all come!"

No matter how much Eddie fumed, Tumen wouldn't stop laughing. In fact, just watching the big man for a few seconds was enough to bring a grin to Clint's face.

"What's so damn funny?" Eddie asked.

Tumen's smile didn't fade in the slightest when he answered that question. "You say you were locked up like an animal. Then you say you were thrown into a pit." Shifting his eyes to Clint, he said, "When the other men came to get him, they found him under Nayan."

"Nayan?" Clint asked. "Is that the woman Chuluun was talking about?"

"Yes."

"That's enough of that," Eddie said. "Can't we just ride in peace?"

"She was riding you good," Tumen said. "His hands were bound and he was squirming like an animal in a trap. Still, she rode him hard enough to scream when she was through. If the bounty hunter didn't like that pit of Nayan's, then perhaps he would like to be tied up with the men."

Clint and Tumen both laughed at that.

"I said that's enough!" Eddie snapped.

"She really screamed?" Clint asked. "I think I heard that."

"The whole camp heard that," Tumen replied.

Clint shook his head and looked over at Eddie. "And here I was feeling bad for handing you over just to avoid us all possibly getting shot. You're right, Eddie. I'm truly ashamed of myself."

Just as Eddie was about to try to salvage some of his pride, Tumen cut in with, "If you get a chance to hand me over to some wild woman who might tie me up and ride me, I think you should do it."

When Clint started laughing this time, he thought he might not be able to stop. "Tell you what, big man. I know a few places in the Territories where I might just be able to hand you over to some very capable women."

"That would be good."

"For a man who just might try to kill us, you're a funny guy, Tumen."

"Yeah," Eddie growled. "Real fucking funny."

THIRTY-TWO

Since they were headed toward Prescott, Clint decided to ride to the stagecoach platform where he'd received Maddy's letter. Since he'd been attacked the last time he was there, he figured it was a good spot to look for a sign of where the gunmen could have gone in the meantime. Eddie Sanchez might have been a whining, thieving pain in the ass, but he was good enough to pick up on something Clint might have missed.

When the platform was in sight, Clint pulled back on his reins and waited for the others to come to a stop. "I think Eddie should do this alone," he said.

Tumen didn't like the sound of that. His face hardened into a suspicious scowl that didn't need any words to go along with it.

As always, Eddie had more than enough words to make up the difference. "Oh yeah. I could use some time to scout on my own. Shouldn't take me more than a few hours to have a look around."

"I'll go with him," Tumen said.

Eddie started to protest, but cut himself short. Arguing with the big man would have done as much good as debating a post.

"All right, then," Clint said. "If any of those men who attacked me before are still lurking about, they shouldn't be expecting either of you two. See what you can find and meet me back here. If you take too long, I'll come in after you."

Both of the men rode toward the platform and Clint watched them go. Once they were far enough away, Lylah's arms tightened around Clint's midsection. He looked over his shoulder and said, "You can go if you want."

"I . . . go?"

"If you want."

Her only response was to hold on to him and press her face against his shoulder in its familiar spot.

"All right then. Where?"

Oddly enough, she understood that portion of a question better than when Clint spoke to her in real sentences. It made sense, considering what little English she knew, but still felt peculiar in practice. Lylah extended a hand around his right arm to give him some of the parchment Chuluun had provided.

Clint looked at the map and said, "I know. We're headed there."

She tapped a finger against a spot on the map that roughly translated to where they were at the moment.

"Yep," Clint said. He pointed at the same spot and then toward the stagecoach platform. "Here is . . . here. You're right."

Lylah's pointing turned into more insistent taps that threatened to knock the map from Clint's hand. He looked down again and noticed she was tracing a line from the platform to the camp where she thought Kyle Morrow could be found.

Just then, a rumbling rattle sounded in the distance. When she spotted the stagecoach rolling down another trail toward the platform, Lylah slapped Clint's shoulder and pointed even more fiercely.

"I see it. So what?" Reminding himself that she didn't

understand, Clint performed the exaggerated shrug that at least conveyed the fact that he didn't understand something.

Lylah pointed to the coach, then to the platform, then traced the line on the map. Finally, Clint felt what he swore was Lylah's forehead knocking against his shoulder.

"Don't get too riled up. I wish Chuluun was here just as much as you do." Just then, Clint wished he had something to knock *his* head against. While the old man might not be there to translate, he'd sent along notes from the long discussion he'd had with Lylah in her native tongue. He'd read through the notes during the night he'd spent in Chuluun's camp, but hadn't committed them to memory. He did recall, however, one particular note that seemed to tie in with what Lylah was trying to tell him now.

Clint found the line he was after without having to sift through too much of Chuluun's chicken scratch handwriting. The section read, "She was taken from a stagecoach bound for California. Morrow took more women from one other coach before she got away from him."

Although he had plenty to ask her, Clint didn't waste any time trying to come up with a gesture to get his point across. Instead, he tapped Lylah's hands, which was the signal they'd worked out for her to hang on. He then snapped his reins and raced to find Eddie and Tumen.

Fortunately, the two men weren't in such a hurry. Clint caught up with them and kept right on going. Sure enough, Eddie and Tumen did their best to match Eclipse's pace. Since the Darley Arabian had built up a head of steam, they didn't stand a chance.

Clint pulled back on his reins only to keep Eclipse from blazing a trail through the shack beside the platform. He and Lylah had developed a good rhythm with each other while in the saddle, so she knew just when to slide down so both of their feet hit the ground at the same time.

"Have you lost any stages recently?" Clint shouted as he marched toward the shack.

The clerk inside the crooked box was already nervous and became even more so when Eddie and Tumen thundered to a stop. "Please don't shoot!" the little man in the stagecoach office said. "I don't have any money!"

"I'm not here to rob you!" Clint said.

The clerk blinked, stretched his head toward the window that looked out of the shed, and replied, "Oh, yeah. I remember you."

"And I," Eddie said as he swung down from his saddle, "remember you. Hello, Lester."

The clerk winced and backed away from the opening. "Hello, Eddie."

"You still tipping off robbers when all the lockboxes are being hauled through here?"

The clerk didn't answer, but he squirmed a whole lot more. For Clint, that was answer enough.

THIRTY-THREE

So it seemed there was more than one reason why the clerk was so squirrelly. Clint was ready to chalk it up to more obvious things like having a man charge up to his little shed while riding a Darley Arabian stallion on a mission. But the clerk had a lot more to worry about than that. Once Eddie began asking more questions, the little man seemed ready to crawl out through a crack in his wall. He wasn't about to answer those questions, however, until Tumen leaned toward the window as if he was going to pull the clerk straight through it.

"I haven't talked to any robbers for months," Lester squealed.

"What about kidnappers?" Clint asked. "Or a kidnapper named Kyle Morrow?"

"His boys were just here not too long ago," the clerk said.

"I know. I was here, too."

"Oh, yeah. That's right."

"Where did they go?"

The stage that had just arrived was rolling to a stop beside the platform and a man was already crawling along the top to pick out certain pieces of luggage. Lester glanced toward the platform, but his attention was brought back to

Clint when he slammed his fist down upon the little piece
of wood protruding just beneath the window.

"Where did they go?" Clint demanded.

"I'm stuck in this damn box all day long! How the hell
should I know?" When Lester started to back away from
the window, Eddie shoved past Clint, reached through the
small opening, and grabbed hold of Lester's shirt.

Pulling the clerk out of his seat until his face knocked
against the edge of the window, Eddie snarled, "Let's see
the lockbox."

"You wanna rob me?"

The longer the three men lingered in front of the shed,
the more other folks took notice. Tumen did a good job of
discouraging anyone from getting too close, but soon there
would be more attention pointed at the shed than Clint would
have preferred.

Eddie, on the other hand, didn't seem to mind. "I ain't
gonna rob a stagecoach company," the bounty hunter said.
"I just asked to see the lockbox."

"Sure," Lester sputtered as he reached directly beneath
his little counter.

"Not that one," Eddie snapped. "The other one. The one
you keep under the floor."

"We need to finish this," Clint said.

"We will, just as soon as I see the other lockbox."

Before Clint could ask just what the hell Eddie was talking about, he heard Lester start to moan like a tortured spirit.

"Jesus, Eddie. Can't we do this when there ain't so many
people around?"

"Sure," Eddie replied as he pulled the clerk so his chest
and his face slammed against the inside of the shed. "I'll
just extract you from your wooden box and we can have a
nice leisurely chat."

"Ow! Dammit!"

"The lockbox. Now."

"You gotta let me go first."

Eddie released Lester, but he set him free with a shove that was hard enough to bounce the skinny man against another wall. "Work fast. If you make me come in there . . ."

But Eddie didn't need to say another word. The clerk scrambled around inside his shed and had returned to the window by the time Clint stepped close enough to get a look inside. Judging by the redness of the clerk's exasperated face, he could very well have been on the verge of tears.

"I can't have anyone at the stagecoach company find out about this," Lester whined. "I can't have anyone around here even see this. The law may be around here, and if—"

"Shut up and open the box," Eddie snapped.

Lester followed his orders and opened the little rectangular box amid the mournful squeal of metal hinges. Inside, Clint could see two stacks of money that must have come to at least a couple hundred dollars.

Eddie nodded and said, "You only get paid when you deliver, Lester. What did you tell them?"

"I didn't—"

"Tell me the truth," Eddie warned. "There's a crowd gathering out here and they want their tickets. It'd be a shame to make them watch as I blow your brains all over them schedules."

Lester turned around to look at the schedules posted behind him and swallowed hard. "I told them about a bunch of men in fancy suits who were on their way to Sacramento."

"That'd be the stage that was robbed last week?" Clint asked. "I read about that."

"I'm sure that's the one," Eddie said. "But that job couldn't have been big enough for your percentage to amount to as much as I see there. You gave them something else."

Clint wasn't inclined to torture a man, but all he had to do was show Lester a scowl and rest his hand upon the grip of his holstered Colt to get things moving again.

"Jesse wanted to know about pretty ladies," the clerk

said, "so I told him about three who had been staying here waiting for the stage bound for Salt Lake City."

Since Lester wasn't about to stray too far from his money, Eddie was able to reach in and grab hold of him again. "Did the stage leave?"

Lester nodded. "Earlier today."

"And it was bound for Salt Lake City?"

Lester nodded again.

Eddie shoved the clerk toward the back of his shed and then scooped out a fistful of money from the lockbox. Turning away, he stalked toward his horse with Clint following behind. "Don't worry, Clint. This ain't the stagecoach's money. Lester watches everyone and everything that passes through here and he tells anyone what he knows, so long as the price is right."

Suddenly, a woman screamed. Clint pivoted on the balls of his feet and saw Lester bring up a shotgun that must have been hidden beneath his window. Tumen ended that threat with a quick jab that went straight through the clerk's window and pounded squarely against his nose. Lester, his shotgun, and even some of his money flew back from the window and landed upon the floor.

The bounty hunter glanced over his shoulder and muttered, "He must've just gotten that shotgun. About time, I suppose."

"So men pay for Lester to tell them which stages to rob?" Clint asked.

"Yeah. How do you think a robber's gonna know which stage is worth the trouble? But Jesse is one of Kyle Morrow's men, and if he knows that there are a few pretty ladies on one stage, he'll run right after 'em."

"But they were after us," Clint explained. "They're after Lylah."

Eddie patted Clint's shoulder and said, "I know how these assholes think. Even if some men are still trying to hunt you two down, Morrow ain't about to miss an opportunity to get a few ladies to sell. Do you know how much something like that's worth? Seein' as how he already paid Lester for the information, I don't see why he wouldn't act on it."

If anyone could think like a piece of shit kidnapper, it was Eddie Sanchez. "All right," Clint said. "Let's go."

THIRTY-FOUR

The trail to Salt Lake City was a long one, and there were bound to be plenty of stops along the way. Fortunately, Clint didn't need to know about every stop. All he needed to keep in mind was that a stage would use the main trails and that it would be headed north. According to Lylah's map, that wasn't exactly the direction in which he needed to go, but Clint wasn't about to let Kyle Morrow's gang steal any more innocent women just for the sake of keeping a schedule.

Eclipse led the way on a race that ran for miles along a barren stretch of the Arizona Territories. Dusty winds scratched Clint's face like a set of jagged nails. A harsh sun glared down at them to scorch the backs of their necks and send rivers of sweat rolling down all three men's faces. Lylah kept her cheek pressed against Clint's shoulder as her hair whipped in every direction.

The longer they rode, the more Clint wondered if he'd made the right decision. Even if Morrow's men were going after a stage, getting to them might not do as much good as getting to Morrow himself. And since Kyle Morrow was the one responsible for killing Madeline Gerard, there was no telling what else he was capable of. Putting a stop to a man like that might just take precedence over going after anyone else.

Clint didn't like it when he had too much time to think about something like that. With nothing but empty trail ahead of him and clear blue sky overhead, his mind was allowed to wander a little too much. That was brought to a stop when he and the others cleared a rise that allowed them to see the next couple of miles stretch out in front of them like a map that had been rolled out and laid upon the floor.

"That's them," Eddie shouted as he waved toward the dust cloud in the distance. "Gotta be!"

Clint shielded his eyes from the sun as he looked ahead. The dust that had been kicked up hung in the sky like a dirty stain, marking the spot where several horses had converged upon a wagon. Judging by the size and shape of that wagon, Clint was certain it was a stagecoach. Rather than try to scream at the bounty hunter over the thunder of the horses' hooves, Clint nodded and tapped his heels against Eclipse's sides. The Darley Arabian poured some more steam into his strides and tore up the trail as if he was on a mission. The other two kept up, but just barely.

Distances might have been hard to gauge in such open country, but Clint, Eddie, and Tumen were riding fast enough to close the gap between them and the stagecoach without much difficulty. With the dust settling around the stagecoach, it was obvious that it was no longer moving. The only problem was that there was no way to get to the stagecoach without being seen from a long ways off. If the horsemen circling the wagon truly did belong to Morrow's gang, that was probably just what they'd been counting on.

Clint still didn't have a good enough view to tell what the other men were doing to the stage or its passengers. Once the rifle shots started whipping through the air around him, he knew those men's intentions weren't good.

THIRTY-FIVE

Although someone was firing a rifle at them, Clint didn't worry too much about being hit until he got closer. Eclipse was doing a good job of running in a crooked line, which made it damn near impossible for anyone to hit him. Eddie and Tumen had already scattered, taking some of the fire along with them.

Clint was so wrapped up in what he was doing that he almost forgot about his passenger. Pulling back on his reins, he extended an arm behind him and said, "Go!"

Lylah understood him well enough to take the arm Clint offered and climb down from the saddle. As soon as her feet touched the ground, she huddled into a ball and wrapped her arms around her knees.

With a sharp yell from Clint and a touch of his boots, Eclipse was off and running. In no time at all, the stallion had regained nearly all the speed he'd lost by taking his short respite. Now that he was free of Lylah's extra weight on his back, Eclipse was able to weave even more sharply as the shots continued to come at him.

As he approached the stage, Clint could already see a few things very clearly. First of all, there were four men on horseback surrounding the wagon. There could have been another covering them from a distance, but the land was so flat that any marksman would either be in plain sight or too far away to be of any concern.

Second, the stagecoach was most definitely being forced to stay put. The two shapes on the ground beside the stage were too big and squirming too much to be anything other than men. Since the front of the stage appeared to be empty, Clint's guess was that those two men were the drivers.

Third, the men who'd stopped the stage knew what they were doing. Two of them remained near the front of the stagecoach to keep the horses under control while the other two were posted on the side next to the door meant for passengers to climb in and out. They had every important angle covered and didn't budge once the lead started to fly.

Having soaked up all of that in the space of a few seconds, Clint motioned for Tumen to circle around the side of the stage opposite the passenger door. He would have given an order to Eddie if the bounty hunter had bothered to look over at him. Instead, Eddie let out a holler and fired back at the stagecoach.

Just when Clint thought he had a chance of surrounding the stage and taking it back from the robbers, things changed. One of the robbers climbed onto the stage's roof, while another pulled himself up into the driver's seat. A few seconds later, the stage lurched forward and started to roll.

Clint drew his Colt and leaned forward over Eclipse's neck. The Darley Arabian moved like a finely tuned machine and charged straight toward the remaining two gunmen without paying any heed to the shots being fired. The closest gunman had dropped to one knee and raised a rifle to his shoulder to take proper aim. With nowhere else to go, Clint had to hope he could close the distance enough to get within pistol range before the other man pulled his trigger. With every second that ticked by, Clint was certain he wasn't going to make it.

Just as the hairs started to go up on the back of Clint's neck, he heard Eddie fire a quick series of shots at the clos-est gunman. The bounty hunter had managed to get ahead of Eclipse, and his aim was good enough to make the rifle-man drop to a prone position before picking Clint from his saddle. There was still one more gunman to consider, but Tumen was keeping him occupied.

The big man raced at the second gunman while letting out a battle cry that filled the air around him. He charged at the gunman at a full gallop, and when he was close enough, swung one leg over and launched himself from his saddle. As he sailed through the air, sunlight glinted from the blade in Tumen's hand.

As much as he wanted to watch the collision, Clint shifted his focus back to the rifleman in front of him. Eddie had managed to distract the man on the ground for a sec-ond, but it was at the cost of drawing the rifleman's fire. Once again proving to be a professional, the rifleman turned and shot at the bounty hunter and then levered in another round.

Clint squeezed off a quick shot, which he knew would sail wide of its target. While he didn't hit the rifleman, Clint did force him to roll away instead of shooting at Eddie.

The bounty hunter forced his horse to a stop and jumped down from his saddle. He snarled like an animal as he pulled his shooting iron from its holster and fired from the hip.

Clint had a clear shot at the rifleman's back, but hesi-tated before taking the shot. Even with the fight having al-ready commenced, he was reluctant to shoot another man in the back. Of course, there were always ways around those sorts of dilemmas.

"Hey, asshole!" Clint shouted.

Rather than turn to face the insult, the rifleman popped up to one knee so he had both Clint and Eddie in his sights. Clint rode right up to him and kicked the rifleman in the shoulder, sending the man rolling to one side. The rifleman recovered quickly enough to aim and fire before Clint could do anything else.

The bullet whipped through the air, shredding Clint's sleeve and digging a bloody trench through his forearm as if it were the talon of a passing hawk. In the time it had taken for him to fire that shot, the rifleman gave Eddie a chance to close in on him. Eddie pounced, introducing the side of his pistol to the side of the rifleman's head.

The second of the two gunmen had put up a bit of a fight, but Tumen made him pay for that mistake. The big man's knife never stopped moving as he carved the gunman up like he was a Christmas goose. With those two well in hand, Clint focused upon the stagecoach. It had built up some speed and was well outside of pistol range, but that wouldn't last very long. Eclipse was still raring to go, and the horse tore after the stage like he'd been shot from a cannon.

THIRTY-SIX

Clint held his Colt in one hand while gripping his reins in the other. As Eclipse raced to catch up with the stagecoach, Clint shifted his weight to accommodate the stallion's every move. He barely had to nudge Eclipse to steer the Darley Arabian one direction or the other. The ride was so seamless that Clint might as well have been doing all the running himself.

One man lay on top of the stage, facing Clint. He held his fire until Eclipse got a little closer and then sent a shot that hissed within inches of Clint's right shoulder. Rather than try to line up a shot of his own, Clint coaxed a bit more speed from Eclipse to pull up within five or ten yards of the stage. From there, he aimed as if he was pointing his finger at his target and cut loose with a few quick shots.

The first shot chipped away the upper edge of the coach.

The second drilled into a piece of luggage the gunman was using for cover, and the third drew blood.

It didn't look like a fatal injury, but it hurt the gunman enough to straighten him up and present a bigger target. By that time, Clint had also moved in a little closer, so hitting his mark was child's play. His bullet caught the gunman in the chest with enough force to knock him off the top of the stage. Considering the rocky ground beneath the coach's wheels, Clint didn't even bother looking back to see if the gunman was going to present any more trouble.

Clint flicked his reins to get a little more speed out of Eclipse, but then tugged them back a little so he could draw up beside the stagecoach without going too far. Just as he was attempting to strike a balance that would keep him away from the man who'd taken over the driver's seat, that same man leaned out to get a look at him.

It was Jesse, the fat man who'd tried to gun Clint down soon after he'd been given Maddy's letter. "Appreciate you comin' back to us," Jesse said as he fired a shot from his .44. "Saves us the trouble of comin' for you!"

Clint didn't need to watch the fat man's face, so he kept a close eye on the gun he carried. By keeping track of the angle of the barrel, he could make a good guess as to where Jesse was aiming. Clint's first guess was good enough to clear a path for one bullet, but he wasn't about to try his luck with many more. Instead, he pulled on his reins so Eclipse dropped back toward the rear of the stage.

Jesse leaned out and fired wildly at Clint. Sooner or later, the fat man would get lucky, and Clint didn't want to be there when he did. In fact, he didn't even want Eclipse to be there. That left him with one good option.

Before he could think better of it, Clint holstered his pistol and rode up a bit closer to the stage. Standing up in one stirrup, he hoisted himself off Eclipse's back so he could jump onto the stage. Clint reached out with both hands to grab the top ridge of the coach. His fingers quickly found something to grip, but his feet weren't having such an easy time as they scraped and bounced off the side of the bouncing carriage.

A few more shots were fired, but they seemed to be wilder than the others. And since they weren't accompanied by any more talk, Clint hoped that Jesse had lost sight of him altogether. Clint lifted one leg to use a ridge on the side of the coach as a toehold. It wasn't much, but it allowed him to pull himself up and onto the roof. Just as he was about to climb all the way up, he saw Jesse look back at him.

"There you are!" Jesse said as he brought a shotgun up to aim at the back of the stage.

Clint had less than a second to keep his head from being blown completely off his shoulders. He used that time to grab the rail that ran along the top of the stage and swing himself over the edge. His fingers locked around the rail with every ounce of strength he could muster. When his arms reached their limit, his entire body slapped against the side of the stage with an impact he felt all the way down to his toes. Clint's shoulders screamed for mercy, but he somehow managed to hang on as the shotgun blast tore a chunk from the section of roof where he'd just been.

Clint dangled from the stage like a flag at half-mast. His fingers burned, but he couldn't tell if they'd been hit by some buckshot or if they were simply about to snap from the pressure of keeping the rest of his body off the ground. It didn't really matter either way. Between the sweat from his hands and possibly blood added to the mix, Clint wasn't going to stay on the coach for long. Every jostling bump that rattled the stage caused him to slip a little farther.

THIRTY-SEVEN

Clint could hear the screeching of his palm sliding against the rail as if it was the only sound on earth. Any second now, he expected to feel his boots knock against the ground. After that, the pain of snapping bones was sure to follow.

Instead of anything so bad, however, Clint felt something entirely different. At first, he thought something had just fallen from the roof to brush against his side. Then he felt something press against his ribs, work its way toward his back, and take hold of his shirt.

"Hang on, mister!" a man from inside the stagecoach said. "I got ya!"

Clint looked down to find a man leaning out through the window of the coach's side door. He must have had someone inside keeping him from falling out, because he stretched out to grab Clint with both hands as if he meant to lift him onto the roof. The man didn't have the strength or the proper angle to do that much, but he steadied Clint against the coach and gave him a few moments to get a better grip.

Once he stopped flapping against the stagecoach, Clint could catch his breath, tighten his hands around the rail, and finally set his toes against something that would allow him to climb back up again. "Thanks, but get back inside," he said.

The other man was hesitant to let go. "Are you sure you won't fall?"

Before he could answer, Jesse leaned over to see what Clint was doing.

"I'm sure," Clint said. "Get in and keep your head down!"

"Yer some kinda goddamn tick!" Jesse said. "We'll just see about that." He began to steer the coach as if he were weaving between telegraph posts. The horses whinnied at the wild tugging of their reins, which only caused the coach to shake more.

But Clint was past the point of being shaken loose. Now that he'd gotten a firm hold, he was able to stay low and work his way onto the roof. Once he was on top of the stage, he had plenty to grab as he slithered toward the driver's seat.

Whenever the coach hit a large enough bump in the road, Clint's entire body lifted off the roof and came back down again with a jolt. Those brief moments allowed him to cover even more ground since his belly wasn't scraping against the top of the coach. By the time Jesse had his shotgun reloaded and turned to look for a target, Clint was close enough to grab the weapon and yank it from the man's hands.

"You're a stubborn fucking tick!" Jesse snarled as he drove a meaty fist into Clint's face.

Clint turned away from the punch to keep his nose from getting busted, but he still caught a good portion of the fat man's knuckles. The moment he felt Jesse try to reclaim his shotgun, Clint rolled onto his side so he could grip the weapon in both hands. He might not have been able to aim it properly, but Clint got one finger on the trigger and pulled it.

The shotgun let out a deafening roar that washed away the sound of the stage's wheels, along with everything else. Neither man was hit by any buckshot, but Jesse's hand had been on the barrel when the gun went off. The scents of singed flesh and burnt powder drifted through the air. As the ringing in Clint's ears eased up, he could hear the fat man screaming in pain.

Rather than waste time trying to fool with the shotgun, Clint threw it away and clambered into the driver's seat. Along the way, he shoved Jesse to one side and gave him a right cross to the chin for good measure.

"If I can't burn a tick out, I can cut him out," Jesse said through a newly bloodied mouth.

Clint collected the reins in one hand and drew his Colt with the other. "Maybe you should sit still before this tick burns a hole through your skull."

Jesse froze with one hand loosely wrapped around the handle of the knife kept in a scabbard at his belt. He glared at Clint with murderous rage, but had enough sense not to act on it. Grudgingly, the fat man lifted his hand away from his knife and slumped into his seat.

"Your men aren't going to help you," Clint said as he wrestled to bring the team under control. "It'd be best if you tell me where you intended on bringing these folks."

"We were just after money and valuables."

The horses were agitated, but Clint was able to convince them to slow down. "That's not what Lester said."

"Who?"

"You know Lester." Clint grunted as he gave the reins another couple of tugs. "Squirrelly guy who tells you which stages have valuables and which have pretty ladies. Seems like you're not the only ones he likes to talk to. And this isn't a stage carrying much in the way of valuables."

Now that the horses had calmed down, they lost even more of their steam. The entire stage rattled to a stop as Jesse let out a tired curse. "Little prick," he said. "I knew we should'a killed him rather than pay his fee."

Clint set the brake and took Jesse's knife away from him. It was a fine blade with an intricately carved handle, so he kept it rather than toss it to join the shotgun in the dirt. "Where were you going to take these people?" he asked.

Jesse chuckled under his breath and shook his head just enough for his extra chins to waggle.

"I already know about the camp that's a few days' ride from here," Clint said. "If you tell me all about that place, I may just let you ride in the wagon when I take you to the law instead of dragging you behind it."

The fat man flinched when he heard that, but didn't say a word.

Clint shrugged. "All right, then. Suit yourself."

THIRTY-EIGHT

It wasn't long before Eddie and Tumen rode up to the parked stagecoach. Several people were gathered around it, talking among themselves to create an excited commotion. When they saw the two new arrivals, they stopped talking and backed away.

"Mister Adams!" a well-dressed man shouted.

Clint poked his head from around the stagecoach and waved at the newly arrived riders. "You're just in time! Our friend here has been very helpful."

Eddie and Tumen dismounted and walked around the stage. They were then treated to the sight of Jesse tied to the spokes of one of the rear wheels by both wrists. He kicked at the ground with both feet and struggled frantically without making an inch of progress. Judging by the thick layer of sweat upon his red face, he'd been doing so for a while.

"What in the hell?" Eddie mused. "We sure missed a lot while dealing with them others."

"Not really," Clint said as he dusted himself off and walked toward the bounty hunter. "Our friend here is full of piss and vinegar, but not much else." Once he got a bit closer, Clint draped an arm around Eddie's shoulders as if conversing with an old friend. "He won't part with any more details of where to find Morrow's camp, but he's let plenty slip."

Eddie looked at the fiercely defiant fat man and asked, "Like what?"

"Like the fact that Morrow and plenty of others will be there. It seems this isn't the first stage the gang has picked off recently, but it was convenient, since they were already there to hunt down Lylah."

"He told you all of that?"

Clint had cobbled those things together once he had figured out which of Jesse's threats had some fact behind them and which were bluffs. Once the fat man became convinced that Clint truly meant to get the stagecoach moving with him attached to it, Jesse's lies became flimsier than wet newspaper. Rather than reveal his tricks to Eddie, Clint nodded and said, "More or less. He seemed pretty confident that we'd run into plenty of gunhands once we got there, so we know a bit of what to expect."

"And what about the rest? You found out there were more prisoners?"

"He sure didn't seem surprised when I told him I already knew about them," Clint explained. "The main thing to keep in mind is that this camp is heavily fortified. We'll either have to sneak in or hire ourselves an army."

"I suppose that's good to know before we get too close to the place." Looking over to the fat man, Eddie asked, "What should we do with him?"

"We can't just leave him here," Clint pointed out.

"Why?" Tumen asked.

Since the big man hardly ever spoke, Clint was a little surprised to hear that single, rumbling syllable. "Because he's a killer and a kidnapper," Clint replied. "He'll probably steal the first horse he can and put down whoever tries to stop him."

"Not if I break his neck."

Eddie chuckled. "He's got a point there."

"No," Clint said. "They're the killers. Not us."

"His legs, then," Tumen said, as if the matter had been decided. "I'll just break his legs. Then he won't go anywhere."

"Wait a second. You're the bounty hunter, Eddie. You must know where to drop him off. Hell, you can even keep the bounty."

Clint wasn't exactly being generous with that offer. He simply didn't want to take the time to do the job himself, and didn't expect Eddie to split the money anyway. To his surprise, the bounty hunter recoiled and seemed to be genuinely offended.

"Why would I keep the bounty?" Eddie asked. "You're the one that brought him down. If there's a price on his head, I know a place where I can collect it, but I'll cut you two in on it. After all, it's only fair."

"Can you do it on your own?" Clint asked.

"He might be a big sack of lard, but he's only one man," Eddie said as he turned to face Jesse. "I can bring him in and meet up with you before you charge into hell, guns blazing."

"Maybe Tumen could go with you."

"No 'maybe,'" Tumen said. "I came to watch him. I won't let him ride anywhere unless I'm watching him."

"Jesus Christ," Eddie groaned.

Clint patted Eddie on the shoulder. "With him riding along, maybe he could carry one of those dead men with him. You think they're worth something?"

"Not unless they're famous," Eddie replied. "Corpses aren't too valuable, Adams."

"Well, I'm not about to talk the big fellow out of anything, so it looks like you're stuck with him. I don't know how long it will be before anyone will miss these men, so I don't want to wait around before hitting Morrow's camp."

"I said I'd catch up to you, and I will," Eddie assured him.

Tumen's hand landed with a heavy thump as it dropped onto Eddie's shoulder. "You mean *we* will."

"We sure will," Eddie said with a grin. "Why would we ever want to miss a foolhardy charge like that?"

"I heard what you assholes are sayin'," Jesse shouted. "Ain't nobody that's been to Kyle's camp is gonna help you. I already told you to shove it up yer ass, and anyone else is too dead to say a damn word." The fat man amused himself with that enough to let out a guffaw that shook his rounded gut. He not only laughed harder when Eddie approached him, but also spat upon the bounty hunter's shirt.

Eddie squatted down to pull the bandanna from around Jesse's neck to wipe off his shirt. He then shoved the slimy cloth down the front of Jesse's shirt as he said, "Hey, Tumen. You want to give me a hand with this greasy bastard?"

The towering Mongolian stomped over to Jesse, grabbed one of his arms, and started pulling as if he wanted to see if it or the wheel would snap first.

"Better let me cut those ropes," Eddie said.

Jesse wasn't laughing anymore as he was loaded onto Eddie's horse. While that was happening, Clint approached the group of passengers who'd gathered a little ways from the stagecoach.

"Is anyone hurt?" Clint asked.

There were five passengers, three of whom were young women who were all beautiful in a similar way. One of the two men was dressed in a black suit and looked to be somewhere in his fifties. The other was the fellow who'd helped Clint hang on to the stage when it had been moving.

The eldest of the women appeared to be in her late twenties and had long, chestnut colored hair. She ran over to Clint and immediately wrapped her arms around him. He was taken by surprise by the embrace, but couldn't help noticing the sweet smell of her as she held on to him. "They were going to take us," she sobbed. "Me, my sisters, all of us. They meant to kill anyone who they couldn't sell. They told us so. I don't know who you are, but thank you. Thank you for coming after us."

Clint could feel the woman trembling against him. When he tried to calm her down, he only felt her grip on him tighten. Both of the woman's sisters wrapped their arms around him as well while the two men helped Eddie and Tumen deal with Jesse. Clint didn't want to waste any time before getting the stagecoach ready to roll, but he let the women gather their strength before parting ways. If they needed to take some of Clint's strength to get them through, then so be it.

THIRTY-NINE

Lylah was waiting right where Clint had left her. In fact, he wouldn't have been surprised if she'd stayed in the same exact spot after he'd dropped her off. She kept her head down until he was close enough for her to be certain it was him. As Eclipse drew up next to her, she stood and patiently waited for Clint to reach down and help her up behind him.

"Tumen and Eddie?" she asked. "They go?"

"They went, but they'll be back." Clint went through a series of hand motions that he hoped would convey that same idea and, thanks to all of his recent practice in that regard, did a decent enough job. "They'll meet us at Tucari."

She seemed perplexed by that last part, so Clint took out Chuluun's map and pointed to the small town marked as the only one close to Morrow's camp. "Here," Clint said. "They'll meet us here."

"Now, we will go?"

Clint turned back around to get a good look at her. "Have you been practicing your English?"

Her face showed some of the confusion she felt when he spoke too quickly, but not as much as usual.

"I know . . . some."

"So you've been holding out on me, huh?"

The confusion returned to her face, answering Clint's question well enough.

"We'll go," he told her. "Then, they'll come to us."

She nodded slowly, but scowled as if she was still sifting through the words in her head to make sense of them. Whether she completely understood or not, she was comfortable enough to settle into her normal spot upon Eclipse's back, wrap her arms around Clint's midsection, and rest her head upon his shoulder.

It would take some hard riding to make up for the time they'd lost in their sidetracking, but Eclipse was always up for a challenge like that. The addition of Lylah might have been a little more weight than the stallion was used to, but she wasn't nearly enough to slow him down much. Clint pressed his hand upon hers until he felt her tighten her grip a little more. Once she was braced, they were off and running.

The stagecoach might have been shot up a little, but it wasn't damaged enough to keep it from getting to its next stop. The drivers were dead, but a few of the passengers were able to take their place. Clint didn't need to worry about them, and he sure didn't need to worry about Eddie. The bounty hunter was just as anxious to get rid of Jesse as he was to take part in the attack on Morrow's camp. Any trouble that Jesse might cause wouldn't slow Eddie down, and it sure wouldn't ruffle Tumen's feathers.

There was always the possibility that Jesse wouldn't make it to a lawman's office, but Clint wasn't about to lose much sleep over that. He had enough faith in Eddie's regard for money to be fairly certain the bounty hunter would get his prisoner where he needed to go. After what he'd seen and heard about the Morrow gang, all of their members had done more than enough to earn their spot in hell, if that's what it came down to.

The rest of the day was spent with nothing but the sound

of hooves pounding against the rocky ground filling Clint's ears. A hot Arizona sun looked down upon him and Lylah as they covered one mile after another to get back on their intended course. After making up for the ground they'd lost by pursuing the stagecoach, Clint forged ahead to get even closer to Morrow's camp.

When he stopped to give Eclipse some rest, Clint filled his canteen at a river and looked over the notes Chuluun had taken while talking with Lylah. The old man was nothing if not thorough, and there was plenty to read upon those pages. Most of what pertained to the location of the camp had already been transferred to the map, but Clint went over it all again just to be sure. He even spoke to Lylah to make sure everything was as complete as possible.

Throughout their time together, he and Lylah had put together a kind of language of their own. Most of it consisted of gestures combined with simple phrases they'd used enough to know front and back. Clint still tried speaking to her normally and, every so often, stumbled upon a word or two that he hadn't realized she knew. There wasn't much for her to add except for a few details about the terrain surrounding Morrow's camp. Just as he was about to give up, she revealed another word she'd learned.

"Man. Here," she said, while pointing at the map to a spot off the trail leading to the camp.

Clint examined the part of the map she was pointing to and asked, "Man?"

She nodded and then pointed to three spaces, one after the other. "Here. Here. Here."

"Oh, you mean lookouts?"

That went a bit further than Lylah's speech could go.

"Men," Clint said as he patted the modified Colt hanging at his side. Furrowing his brow while taking hold of the gun, he asked, "Men with guns?"

Lylah shook her head and walked over to Eclipse. The

Darley Arabian was plenty familiar with her and barely stirred from his drinking when she patted the boot hanging from his saddle. "Men with . . ."

"Rifles," Clint told her as he stood beside her and touched the rifle in the saddle's boot.

She nodded and smiled.

"Now that *is* helpful. You really kept your eyes open while you were there. Then again, I suppose you would have. It must have been frightening to . . . Aw, never mind. Thanks."

He was certain she knew that last word, but she still didn't seem to respond to it. Instead, her smile had taken on a more wistful quality as she moved her hand gently beneath the spot where Clint had laid his own upon the rifle's stock. When Clint turned that hand around so he could brush his fingertips against her wrist, she averted her eyes and moved her hand away.

There wasn't a lot of sunlight left, so Clint coaxed Eclipse from the river, climbed onto his back, and helped Lylah up behind him. She kept a tight grip upon him, but wasn't as relaxed during the rest of the day's ride. Whenever she did lean against his back, she felt as taut as a bowstring.

Since they still had a ways to go, Clint let the matter be.

FORTY

Clint wanted to keep riding even though he knew it would still be another day or two before they arrived at the camp. On top of that, no matter how much Lylah added to the map, they would still undoubtedly have to search around a bit before they actually found the place. The map was a help, but it only put them in the vicinity. After that, Clint would need to rely on everything from tracking skills to pure gut instinct. Somehow he knew he'd be able to smell all those murdering bastards when he got close enough.

He thought about that as he prodded the fire that he had built beside a small cluster of rocks that he'd chosen as the spot to make their camp for the night. Before he was distracted for much longer, he threw the twig he'd been holding into the crackling flames and stood up. "You hungry?" he asked.

Lylah was nearby, dipping her feet into a little watering hole a few yards from the fire. While the Arizona Territories might feel like rocky desert in places, Clint had spent enough time there to know where to look for the essentials. This spot was so nice that he decided he ought to remember where it was for the next time he passed through. Then again, it wasn't exactly the terrain that made the spot easy on the eyes.

Lylah had progressed from dipping her feet to stripping down and submerging herself in the water. Her clothes lay in a dirty heap beside the water near where Eclipse was tethered. She was a few paces in with the water lapping at the upper curve of her breasts while she splashed more of it upon her face and into her hair.

After standing there watching her for a few moments, Clint cleared his throat. "Are you hungry, Lylah?"

She was facing away from him, but quickly turned to look toward the sound of Clint's voice. When she saw him standing there, she gazed up from the water and slowly let her hands drift down along the front of her body. Although she was mostly submerged, the shape of her naked figure and the dark color of her nipples could be seen through the water.

"You . . . uh . . . want to eat?" Clint asked.

Lylah nodded. She must have been kneeling in water that wasn't as deep as it seemed, because she rose from it like an offering. Her body was thin and covered in the sheen of wetness. Her hair clung to her shoulders as droplets trickled from it to slide between her pert little breasts and form a stream that flowed down along her flat stomach. After only a few seconds of the night air, her penny-sized nipples became hard. She looked down at her body, but didn't make a move to cover herself.

Suddenly, as if she'd just snapped out of a deep sleep, she turned and crossed her arms over her chest. Even though she was covering her front, Clint was still treated to the fine view of her back. The water came to just below her waist, allowing him to see the gentle line of her spine, which guided his eyes straight to the tight curve of her buttocks.

Clint might not have understood her language, but he could tell she was feeling uncomfortable. If he could have talked to her, he might have tried to get closer to her. As it was, he didn't know if she'd changed her mind completely about something or if she just needed a bit of coaxing. Considering how much she'd already been through, Clint decided not to push her any more.

"Here you go," he said as he picked up her dress and held it out to her. The breeches she wore under her skirt remained on the ground, but he left them there until she told him otherwise.

Lylah turned to look at him over her shoulder. Realizing she was still halfway out of the water, she lowered herself back down and then turned around again. He could still get an eyeful through the rippling water, and she didn't seem to mind that at all. When she made her way over to him, Lylah smiled sheepishly and reached up to take the dress from his hand. Her breasts came up a bit from the water, but she quickly dropped down again.

There was plenty Clint wanted to do, but taking advantage of a woman wasn't one of them. He'd felt a kinship with Lylah despite the fact that they couldn't have a real conversation. Actually, he felt closer to her because of all the effort it took to express the simplest thing.

"If you want me, you know where to find me," he said.

Lylah didn't say anything, but she did shoot him a quick glance over her shoulder. After that, she turned her back to him and dunked her dress into the water so she could wash out some of the dirt.

After a few seconds of waiting, Clint began to feel awkward. She was washing her clothes and seemed to have forgotten he was there. Cursing at one hell of a missed opportunity, Clint walked back to the fire.

FORTY-ONE

All evening and into early night, Clint kicked himself for not grabbing hold of the chance he'd been given. The more he thought about it, the more he felt like an awkward boy who'd been too bashful to ask a pretty girl to dance. He was not a nervous boy and Lylah was not a little girl, which made the misstep even more grating. Even worse was the fact that he couldn't just go over to her as if nothing had happened. Every moment that passed, the trail just got colder. At least, that's what he felt until Lylah came to him.

Dinner had been a quiet affair, followed by a quick retreat to his bedroll. Clint had offered the bedroll to her, but Lylah was more comfortable closer to the fire, wrapped up in his jacket. Clint lay on his side, trying to get some sleep, when he heard the faint rustle of movement drawing closer. Before he could shift and get a look for himself, he felt a lithe, warm body slip into place beside him.

Lylah eased in with Clint as simply as the many times she'd climbed up to sit with him in the saddle. This time, however, she was able to drape an arm and leg over his side as she nestled in against him.

Having intended to get some sleep, Clint had already stripped off his boots. When he rolled onto his other side to face her, Clint felt the warm touch of Lylah's bare breasts against his chest. She was lying naked beside him, watching him with wide eyes as if there was a chance in hell that he might disapprove.

Clint allowed his eyes to wander along the front of her body. Lylah's skin was dark enough to look as if she'd spent almost too much time in the sun. Her breasts were just small enough to remain pert, even when she was lying on her side. The dark nipples were soft at first, but instantly became rigid the moment Clint placed a hand upon her.

Lylah let out a shuddering sigh and closed her eyes. The smile on her face told him that she'd probably been waiting for that moment almost as long as he had. Her skin was just as soft as it looked. After brushing a hand along the side of her breasts, Clint moved it over her side, along the gentle slope of her hip, and as far down her leg as he could reach. He propped himself up so he could reach a little farther to move the palm of his hand along the tight curve of her backside.

When Clint eased his hand along the back of her thigh, Lylah moaned softly and moved her legs apart. The thatch of hair between them was still a little wet from her bath, but the dampness Clint felt when he explored her further came from anything but water. He watched her face change as he moved his hand from the tender nub of her clitoris to the silky skin of her inner thigh. When he reached between her legs again and eased a finger between the lips of her pussy, Lylah began speaking her own language in a fluid cascade of moaning sighs.

Clint might not have known what she was saying, but he got the intent well enough. Their bodies were doing all the talking that needed to be done. When he started to move his hand away from her, Lylah took hold of it and guided it once more between her thighs. When Clint rubbed her faster down there, she opened her legs wider and groaned louder.

He could feel her climax approaching through the trembles in her muscles all the way down to the curl of her toes. Lylah quickly rolled onto her back, spread her legs wide, and placed her hand on top of his so she could guide him through the last few motions needed to push her over the edge. Clint didn't need much help in that regard, but it was exciting to let her do what she pleased.

Lylah didn't care how she looked or how she sounded. All she wanted was to squeeze every last bit of pleasure she could out of the next few moments. When her orgasm finally came, her eyes snapped open and she turned to look at Clint. The expression on her face shifted a few times as he moved his hand and fingers in a few ways she hadn't been expecting. When she let out the breath she'd pulled in, her entire body shrank down.

Since it looked as if she didn't have the strength to get up, Clint got to his knees and positioned himself between her legs. Lylah tugged at his jeans, loosening them and then pulling them down as far as she could. He finished the job for her and kicked them off, then knelt once more in his spot.

Now it was Lylah's turn to let her hands wander. Although she moved her fingertips along Clint's chest and down his arms, her eyes never left his rigid penis. She gazed at it hungrily, and when her hands drifted below his waist, she seemed hesitant to go any farther.

"No need to be shy now," Clint said.

Lylah looked up at his face for a moment, but quickly shifted her eyes back to her real target.

Finally, Clint took her hands the way she'd taken his earlier and moved them to his rigid pole. Judging by her initial reaction, Clint thought he might have been the first naked man she'd ever seen. That possibility was dismissed the moment she started stroking him.

Her fingers curled around his erection and slid slowly up

and down its length. With her other hand, she reached between her legs to rub the wetness of her pussy. She then used that hand to stroke Clint some more, lathering her own juices on him while stroking him faster and more vigorously.

"Damn," Clint gasped. "That's . . . Damn!"

She handled his cock expertly, smiling as he grew harder in her grasp. Clint couldn't take too much more of that before he moved in closer and pushed her legs apart a bit more. Lylah responded by guiding his cock between her thighs and lifting her backside up off the ground a bit so she could meet him halfway.

When Clint felt the tip of his penis brush against her pussy, he thought he might be in for a quick night. She was so wet and so soft that entering her was even better than he'd imagined. To make matters even more difficult to bear, she cinched tightly around his cock so he could feel every glorious second of pushing deeper and deeper into her.

Clint lowered himself on top of her and buried his cock in as far as it would go. Staying there for a second, he was able to collect his thoughts. Just when he was under control, he felt one of Lylah's legs brush against his side while the other slowly encircled his waist. She watched him with tired eyes, as if she needed a second to compose herself as well.

Those few seconds of looking down at her were all Clint required. He started moving slowly in and out of her, watching the intensity build within Lylah's eyes. When he quickened his pace, Lylah wrapped both legs around him and grabbed his shoulders so she could feel the movements of his muscles as he shifted on top of her.

Clint propped himself up with both arms and then straightened so he was once again kneeling between her legs. But Lylah didn't release him. She kept her ankles locked at the small of his back and stretched both arms up over her head.

Clint placed his hands upon her breasts, savoring the feel of her hard little nipples scraping against his palms as he pumped into her again and again.

Lylah unwrapped her legs from around him and scooted back. She then got onto her knees and pushed Clint back just enough for him to sit down with his legs stretched out in front of him. From there, she climbed into his lap, facing him, and shifted until her legs were once more wrapped around him and his cock was pressing against the wet lips of her pussy. A few more subtle motions was all it took for him to enter her. She straddled him, grinding her hips intently while rubbing her hands against Clint's back.

They spent the rest of the night like that, shifting from one position to another, resting when necessary and starting up again when the time was right. Not once did a single word have to pass between them.

FORTY-TWO

The following day passed as if nothing else was going on in the world around them. Clint and Lylah awoke under the same blanket, wrapped in each other's arms, and set about making breakfast and then breaking camp. There was no way for them to get anywhere near Kyle Morrow's camp that day, so all that remained was to ride.

Eclipse was glad for the chance to run for so many miles at a stretch, and Clint enjoyed the chance to feel the wind against his face. Lylah was perfectly content to sit in the saddle behind him, keeping her arms locked tight around his midsection and even squeezing her knees around him. Every so often, her hands would wander down his stomach and below his waist. Clint did his best to keep going, but her little hands were just the right size to stroke him as they rode. Eventually, Clint's erection became too hard to bear, so he found a spot where he could let Eclipse graze while he lifted Lylah's skirt and gave her what she wanted.

Every time they made love, she became bolder. It soon got to the point where Clint thought he would have to deny her advances so they could cover more ground for the day. But she knew just how to get him riled up enough to stop somewhere and indulge her.

Clint didn't even try to place the blame of any delay on her shoulders alone. If he'd wanted to keep riding, he would have been able to do so. What he enjoyed the most was the fact that Lylah was so persistent. When he felt her hands grow restless yet again, he turned and said, "Enough's enough. If we don't ride farther today, we'll just have to go farther tomorrow."

She continued to reach for him, so Clint said, "We're not on a holiday, you know. We need to find Morrow's camp."

Lylah understood that name if nothing else. Although her hands remained where they were, she wasn't rubbing him any longer. Her lips pressed against his ear and she whispered, "Why wait?"

Clint wanted to argue with her, but didn't have it in him.

He wanted to keep riding, but knew she had a point. They really hadn't stopped any more than they normally would throughout a day's ride. Even if they kept riding without pause, it would take at least another day before they reached the hills marked upon Chuluun's map. Lylah's directions weren't exact, but she remembered well enough how long she and Maddy had ridden to get to that stage platform. Clint looked around again and couldn't see any terrain matching what Lylah had described to the old Mongolian man.

While Clint was thinking about all of this, Lylah was still doing her best to tempt him, and Eclipse was tearing along a stretch of broken trail that would hopefully trim some time off their ride. That's when Clint remembered that getting to Morrow's camp too quickly wasn't necessarily a good thing. If he didn't allow for a bit of extra time for Eddie and Tumen to catch up, he'd be storming into that den of killers alone. That, quite simply, wouldn't be very smart.

"Good enough reason for me," Clint said as he brought Eclipse to a stop.

He swung down from his saddle, helped Lylah down, and then led her to the first place she could brace herself as he lifted her skirt and pulled down her breeches. Lylah was surprised by the sudden change of plan, but was more than willing to go along with it.

It wasn't too much longer before they were off and running again. With all the stops here and there, Eclipse was able to gallop at full steam for longer stretches of time. In the end, they wound up covering just about as much ground as Clint had set out to at the beginning of the day.

One other result from all of Clint's and Lylah's distractions was that they were both too tired to do much of anything once they finally made camp. After nightfall, they sat in front of a fire that was too small to attract much attention from any distance, and shared a simple meal.

They undressed and climbed into Clint's bedroll, but didn't do much more than that. Clint enjoyed the feel of her naked body against his, and the way she would occasionally shift in her sleep. Her firm little backside pressed against him in a way that might have been tempting if he hadn't been so damn tired.

Clint wound up getting one of the best night's sleep he'd had in a long time. Considering what lay ahead of him, that was just what he needed.

FORTY-THREE

When Clint awoke the next morning, he felt rested and was raring to go. Being that much closer to Kyle Morrow's camp must have affected Lylah as well, because she was anxious and nervous from the start. Her eyes were already open when Clint woke up, and she didn't say a word throughout the first portion of the day.

That was when Clint had to remind himself that she really didn't say much of anything at any time. They'd just gotten so close that he could feel the nervousness coming off her like heat from a rock that had been dug from the bottom of a brazier. She carried herself as if she wanted to curl up and crawl away somewhere. Judging by how tightly she clung to him, Lylah wanted to take Clint right along with her.

Late that afternoon, the flat desert terrain gave way to rocky slopes and jagged peaks covered in thorny scrub, which more closely matched the land that Lylah had described to Chuluun. Pulling on the reins, Clint looked back at her and asked, "Any of this look familiar?"

She was quiet, so Clint held up the map, pointed to it, and then pointed at the land in front of them. That was good enough to get his question across, so she nodded. More than that, she reached out to point to the town that had been written there as one of the few genuine landmarks Clint could use.

Since he seemed to be headed in the right direction, Clint rode on until he spotted the first signs of civilization.

Actually, calling the town of Tucari "civilization" was being mighty generous. It was a collection of dusty, run-down buildings that had a wild feel to it even though there were no fights in the streets or gunshots to be heard. At least, there were none of those things going on at the moment. Everything from the bawdy voices that drifted out of the town's half dozen saloons to the ragged appearance of the drunks glaring at Clint from the street made Tucari a natural home for outlaws.

Clint only had to spend a few moments in the town to guess that whatever law there might be was not to be trusted. He also felt safe in assuming that he could buy damn near anything from one of the shady characters watching him ride down the street, and that he didn't want to take his hand too far away from his gun.

When Lylah pointed toward a saloon at the next corner, Clint said, "I don't think you want to go into any of these places."

Whether she understood every word or not, she wasn't happy when Clint steered Eclipse toward another street. She pointed insistently at the corner he was about to leave behind and said, "Go there," along with several other words in her own language.

"You sure about that?" Clint asked.

Lylah kept pointing, and since one place didn't look much better than another, Clint played along. He turned Eclipse around and rode toward that saloon she'd been so anxious to visit. When he brought the Darley Arabian to a stop in front of the place, he felt some more taps upon his shoulder.

"See? I told you that you wouldn't want to go there."

But Lylah wasn't pointing at the saloon, and she wasn't

trying to get him to leave. Instead, she pointed to the saloon's neighbor, which was the darkened storefront of a barbershop. Although it was obvious the shop was closed for business, Clint could see light and movement coming from the rooms directly above it. Suddenly, Lylah cupped her hand to her mouth and shouted something at the upper floor.

"We need to keep quiet," Clint insisted. "Quiet! Understand?"

She swatted his shoulder and was about to shout once more, but held back once someone on the second floor peeked out through the window.

The face that looked down at the street from above the barbershop was small, round, and framed by a brightly colored scarf. Clint could barely see more than that before the face disappeared inside again. Moments later, a side door flung open from the top of a narrow staircase that led from the second floor down to the alley between the barbershop and saloon. A stout woman practically exploded from the doorway, climbed halfway down, and began chattering in Lylah's native language.

Lylah hopped down from the saddle and ran for the stairs. Clint followed her, making sure to bring Eclipse into the alley far enough to make it difficult for someone to try to run off with him.

"Who is that?" Clint asked. When he didn't get an answer, he shifted his eyes to the woman and asked, "Ma'am? Who are you?"

After chattering for a bit more, the woman stroked Lylah's cheek and wrapped her up in a big hug. She then looked at Clint and said, "I am called Mother. It's not my name, but good enough for now."

"I'm Clint Adams. I take it you already know Lylah?"

"Yes, I do," Mother replied. Her smile was missing a few teeth, but was bright enough to eclipse the colors dyed into the scarf that was wrapped over her head and tied beneath her chin. "Madeline came here sometimes to help girls like this one get away from here. Is Madeline with you?"

"No, ma'am. Madeline's gone."

"Where did she go?"

"She's dead."

Clint's bluntness was the best test he could have possibly given the older woman. His words brought a shocked sadness to Mother's face that couldn't have been an act. Tears immediately trickled from her eyes as she held Lylah at arm's length and asked her a question in the language they shared.

Lylah spoke softly and nodded while smoothing back some of the hair that had come loose from the older woman's scarf.

Mother steeled herself with a deep breath and asked, "She was killed?"

"Yes, ma'am."

"Was it the kidnappers who are camped outside of town?"

"Afraid so. They caught up to her in Tombstone."

That caused Mother to bring a hand up to her face and press it against her mouth. After lowering her hand a few inches, she gasped. "Then it is my fault. I should never have let her out of my sight. I tell Madeline she does dangerous work, but she keeps doing it. I should never have helped her."

Clint stepped forward to place a hand upon Mother's back. Since Lylah wasn't about to move aside, the three of them huddled together to shut out the rest of the filthy little town. "It wasn't your fault. Both you and Madeline were just trying to do the right thing."

"You are here now to hunt those kidnappers?" Mother asked.

"Yes, ma'am."

"Then you are doing the right thing, too."

"Do you know if those kidnappers are here in town?" Clint asked.

Mother nodded. "They come to saloons to drink. Some of them were here last night. Not all of them, though."

"Yeah, I already caught up to a fat man and three of his partners."

Nodding once again, Mother said, "The fat one left days ago. He is dead now?"

"He won't be coming back. Do you know how many kidnappers there are?"

"I have seen five or six with the man who leads them. His name is Morrow. I saw Morrow last night, but I don't know much more than that. All I do is watch from my window and hope those men don't come to my shop. Now I wish I could do more."

"How about looking after Lylah for a few days," Clint said. "Could you do that?"

"Yes."

Handing over a little more than twenty dollars, he asked, "Is there a stage that comes through here, or maybe a train station nearby?"

"A stage comes through once a week."

"Then use this money to buy her a ticket. Keep whatever's left. If you need more for—"

"No," Mother said sharply. "I only take some to buy ticket, but you keep the rest. Madeline was a good girl. This is a good girl," she added while rubbing Lylah's arm. "I will help because of that, not because of money."

"You're a good girl, too," Clint said before kissing Mother on the cheek.

The old woman grinned and patted Clint's face in turn. "Don't do anything foolish. Don't get hurt."

"Can't promise that, ma'am." Before Mother tried to talk him into staying any longer, Clint tipped his hat and walked back to Eclipse.

Lylah rushed over to him and wrapped her arms around him tightly. It wasn't a surprise that they didn't need to say anything else to each other. She looked into Clint's eyes, placed her hands upon his face, and gently kissed him. She knew where he was going and that he wouldn't be coming back. She also wanted him to be safe and to remember her fondly.

It was a lot to pack into a few seconds, but Clint got the message just fine.

"You expecting someone?" Mother asked.

Clint reflexively put Lylah behind him so he could face whoever was coming without her getting between them. But there were no drunks approaching the barbershop. At least, Tumen didn't look drunk. Eddie, on the other hand, looked a little too happy, considering the circumstances.

"I like this place!" the bounty hunter said.

"Well, I hope you got your fill of it," Clint replied. "Because we're leaving. Did you get any money for the fat man?"

"A bit. Seems he was wanted for a bank robbery. Who knew that lard-ass could run fast enough to get away from anyone? We rode in from the south and I think I saw Morrow's camp. It's a definite possibility anyway."

Clint climbed into his saddle. "If it's not, we'll turn over every rock until we find where Morrow is hiding. I don't care what it takes. This is his last day as a free man."

FORTY-FOUR

Now that they knew where to look, it wasn't difficult at all to find Kyle Morrow's camp. The map Chuluun had drawn was accurate enough to point Clint, Eddie, and Tumen in the right direction, so they continued that way until they found the spot Eddie had mentioned. From a distance, the camp might have been mistaken for a junk heap.

Clint peered through his spyglass to discover the piles of broken wood surrounding the large campfire were actually stagecoaches, carriages, and a few smaller carts that had been dragged to form a crude circle. It was getting dark, but the fire threw enough light onto the shells of cracked wood for Clint to tell they'd barely made it through the rocky pass to what had to be their final resting place. The broken coaches weren't in good enough condition to make a comfortable settlement, but they did a good enough job of sheltering the men in the camp from the elements.

"If they're holding prisoners," Eddie said, "they'd be in that big coach in back."

"They're holding prisoners?" Clint asked.

"They're kidnappers, ain't they? They gotta have a spot to hold their prisoners until a ransom is paid or until they used all the women up."

Clint lowered the spyglass and glared at Eddie.

The bounty hunter shrugged and said, "I ain't the one to kidnap anyone. You think a man like Kyle Morrow just keeps them ladies around to play tag?"

Placing the spyglass to his eye again, Clint continued to study the camp. Sure enough, the coach at the back of the circle was in better condition than the others. Its windows were also boarded up and its door was kept shut by a thick piece of timber wedged between it and the ground. "I only count four men in the camp."

"The rest might'a gone into town," Eddie said. "If we sneak in now, we might be able to get the drop on them."

"Unless it's a trap," Clint pointed out. "I hate to trust something that looks too good to be true."

"They won't be expecting us," Tumen said. "Isn't that why we've worked so hard to find this place?"

"The big fella's got a point," Eddie said. "They wanted to hunt down that pretty lady of yours because she knew how to get here and could lead someone back to them. They killed that other lady for the same reason. Since we're here, let's show them why they needed to be so afraid of them two ladies."

Clint put the spyglass into his saddlebag. "I like the way you think."

The three of them rode toward the camp as if they had every right to be there and no reason to fear the men guarding its perimeter. Two men stood at the spot where the sorry excuse of a trail met up with the broken wagons. One of them let out a series of whistles, but as soon as they got a look at Clint and Eddie, they raised rifles to their shoulders.

Clint brought up his Colt to point it at the closest guard. He pulled his trigger a split second before his two partners followed suit. Clint's round hit the rifleman in the chest and knocked him off his feet. Just to be sure, Clint swung down from his saddle and put a second round into the fallen guard.

The man posted at the other side of the trail fired a shot, but it was done in a rush and hissed through the air between Clint and Eddie. He didn't get a chance to fire again, since the bounty hunter spun him around with a quick shot to the left shoulder. Before the guard could regain his footing or fall over, Tumen rode up and threw his knife at him.

The long blade turned once in the air and landed in the guard's chest with a solid *thunk*. Dropping his rifle, the guard looked down at the knife protruding from him and gasped without making a sound. Tumen stepped forward to reclaim his weapon amid a spray of blood. Once the knife was removed from where it had landed, the guard could only drop and feel his life pour out of him.

Clint had his eyes set upon the wagon near the back of the camp. Between him and that wagon, there were two armed men. Both of them were reaching for their guns

At that moment, everything seemed to slow to a crawl. Clint walked with grim resolve into the glow of the campfire. He barely felt the ground beneath his feet since his mind was full of so many different images. He thought about Maddy's sweet face and then recalled the image of her grave. He thought about Lylah's tears as well as the touch of her hands upon his cheek. When he heard the women screaming for help from within the large wagon that Eddie had singled out, Clint had heard enough.

"Let them go!" Clint demanded.

Both of the armed men were on their feet, holding their guns, a second or two from putting them to use. One man had raised his shotgun, and the other man's pistol was just shy of clearing leather. Since Tumen had taken position to Clint's right, they now had more than one target to choose from.

"Let who go?" the man with the pistol asked.

But the shotgun holder was thinking a bit clearer. "You mean the fancy bitches? I can give you a turn with one of 'em, if you like. That should keep you busy for the last few seconds of yer life."

Eddie had spent the last few moments creeping around the outside of the camp so he could get a look into the large wagon. When he pulled one of the boards away from a window on the side facing away from the fire, the creaking, splintering sound tore through the air.

"Stop!" Clint shouted as the man with the shotgun turned in response to Eddie's commotion. "Throw down your weapons," Clint said." Last chance. Either way, the prisoners are coming with us."

"The hell they are!" the pistoleer said. His words set his partner off as well, and both of them followed through on the motions they'd started just a few moments ago.

Being closer to the pistoleer, Clint focused on him first. As he fired three times in quick succession, he concentrated on making certain no bullets tore through a wagon where more prisoners might be kept. Each of his rounds found its mark, launching the pistoleer into a twitching dance that ended with him slamming against the wagon before sliding to the ground.

Tumen rushed at the man guarding the prisoners. Either he wanted to keep from shooting into the large wagon or he just liked that knife of his, because he ran straight at the shotgunner without making a move toward the gun hanging at his side. The guard panicked and fired his shotgun into the dirt as Tumen got to him. After that, the bigger man's knife found a home in the shotgunner's guts.

Clint kicked out the board wedged against the wagon's door and pulled it open. Seven women and one old man were huddled in the shadows, staring out at him as if they were too frightened to move. "Come on," Clint said as he extended a hand to them. "You're going home."

FORTY-FIVE

It was hours before Clint heard the sound of horses approaching the camp. Those hoofbeats were followed by a series of whistles similar to the ones given by the guards earlier that night. Ignoring what must have been a signal, Clint stood up from where he'd been waiting and placed his hand upon the grip of his holstered Colt.

"Wake up, Georgie!" someone shouted. "Get yer dick out of them ladies and line 'em up. I don't know which one I want yet."

Clint recognized the first horseman as Ayden—the man whose trigger finger he'd snapped back at the stagecoach platform. As soon as Ayden rode close enough for the firelight to touch his face, Eddie sent a rifle round straight through his skull.

The remaining horsemen scattered and fired wildly toward the camp.

"What the hell?" another man asked.

The next voice was strong enough to cut through the chaos and silence all but a few last shots. "Don't shoot till you see who you're shootin' at. Anyone kills one'a them women, they best compensate me for what they're worth."

Clint shook his head and planted his feet, grateful that

the kidnappers had announced their intent as well as their presence.

Now that the gunshots had tapered off, the sound of cautious footsteps could be heard. They encircled the camp and closed in like a snare. When Clint heard someone approaching the wagon where he waited, he shifted his eyes and watched as the figure moved in closer. Whoever it was had his gun drawn and was slowly bringing it up to take good aim at Clint. Before the figure could raise its gun any more, Tumen lunged from the shadow where he'd been crouched and lopped the man's gun hand off with one swipe of his extended blade.

The gunman dropped to one knee, gasping in shock at the loss of his hand. That gasp became a wet gurgle as Tumen dragged his blade across the kidnapper's throat.

"Who's there?" another man asked as he inched cautiously toward the camp while keeping his shoulder pressed against the wagon that was closest to the trail.

"You'd be Kyle Morrow?" Clint asked.

The cautious man squinted toward the fire over the barrel of his pistol. "You got that right. Who're you? The law?"

Clint stepped out from the thick pool of shadow between the now-empty prisoner wagon and the other one at the rear of the camp. "I came for the prisoners. That's all you need to know."

"Looks like you already got 'em." Morrow said.

"I'll give you one chance to drop your guns so I can haul you and what's left of your men to jail."

"Really? Ain't that just sweet of you."

"It's more of a chance than you gave Madeline Gerard."

"Oh, you mean that bitch I gutted in Tombstone? I suppose you're right about that."

Clint pulled in a breath and surveyed the camp. Kyle Morrow was a skinny man with a sunken face and a mustache that looked more like a fungus that had taken root under his nose. His stringy brown hair hung down from a dirty bowler hat that had a feather stuck in the band. Two other men lingered at the camp's perimeter, one of whom was soon dropped by a rifle shot that came without warning.

"Took too long," Eddie said from the roof of the wagon that was on the opposite side of the fire from the one the prisoners had occupied.

That left one more man to stand with Kyle Morrow. Since Tumen was nowhere to be seen, they must have figured it was as good a time as any to make their move.

Morrow already had his pistol drawn, so he shifted his arm to aim at Clint. Without so much as a flinch in the corner of one eye to mark the moment, Clint fired from the hip and clipped Morrow through the ribs. From there, Clint dropped to one knee and fired again.

Morrow's last surviving partner meant to shoot as well, but was having trouble breathing, thanks to the huge knife sticking out of his chest. Clint hadn't seen the knife get thrown, but he did catch sight of a large figure to his left approaching the fire. Ignoring everything else around him, Tumen approached Morrow's partner to finish him off and take back his favorite weapon.

To his credit, Morrow kept his focus where it needed to be. He fired at Clint, but missed due to his haste and Clint's shifting stance. Before he could lower his aim, Morrow caught another one of Clint's rounds in the chest. Morrow gritted his teeth through that, just as he'd fought through the other hits and kept firing.

Clint stood up and saved his final round. Morrow was hurt and starting to fade, which meant his shots were being dragged farther and farther from their mark. When Morrow's hammer fell upon the back of an empty bullet casing, his barrel was pointed at the fire. Even as he staggered back and plopped onto his ass, Morrow was digging under his jacket for another pistol stuck under his belt.

After taking careful aim, Clint sent his last bullet through Kyle Morrow's face and scattered pulpy brain matter across the wagon behind him.

As the last rumble of gunfire echoed into the night, a steely wind blew through the camp. The breeze fanned the flames of the campfire, bringing a few pops from the cinders.

Eddie grunted as he clambered down from atop his perch. Clint saw tentative fingers scraping at the dirt beneath that same wagon.

"It's all right," Clint said while reloading his Colt. "You can come out now."

The prisoners crawled out from beneath the wagon, but looked as if they wanted to go right back under there when they saw the gruesome scene before them. The old man looked up at Clint and said, "They keep their money over there."

Eddie looked over at the smallest of the broken-down wagons before running over to it. After a few seconds, he let out a happy yelp and said, "There's a bunch of saddlebags in here." There was some more rustling, followed by even more joyous whoops. "Sure as shit! They're stuffed full of money!"

"It's ransom money paid for some of the other girls they kidnapped," the old man said. "Those bastards kept it and never returned anyone to their families."

"How many bags are there, Eddie?" Clint shouted.

"Six! All stuffed with—"

"Take one for yourself and give one to Tumen. Hand the rest over to these folks."

The bounty hunter looked positively appalled when he stuck his head out of the wagon. Tumen had taken position just outside the broken doorway, which made Eddie's task a little easier. When the saddlebag was handed out to him, Tumen took it and looked inside.

"Is there enough in there to make up for what was taken from your people?" Clint asked.

Tumen grinned and nodded.

"Then we're done and Eddie can go. Thanks for your help, big man."

After gripping Clint's hand in a friendly shake, Tumen walked back to his horse.

"The rest goes to these people, Eddie. See to it."

One by one, Eddie tossed out four saddlebags. Then the bounty hunter climbed out of the wagon, carrying another bag over his shoulder. "Hardly seems fair," he chuckled.

"Morrow's carcass is worth a pretty penny," Clint said. "He's all yours, along with whoever else you want to drag away from here. You'll hand over some of that cash to me to make up for my portion of the work, and the rest goes to these folks that Morrow wronged. Seems fair to me."

"No, that's not what I meant," Eddie replied as he stuck his hand into the saddlebag and pulled out a wad of cash. Handing it over to Clint, he said, "I mean these assholes. Putting them down was like shooting fish in a barrel. I ain't complaining, but still . . ."

Clint flipped through the cash and found more than he'd expected. Stuffing the money into his pocket, he looked at the crumpled form of Morrow's corpse and growled, "These bastards didn't deserve a fair fight."

Watch for

PLEASANT VALLEY SHOOT-OUT

338th novel in the exciting GUNSMITH series
from Jove

Coming in February!

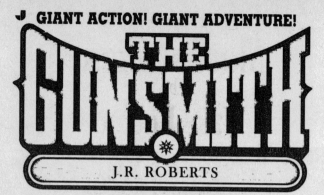

GIANT ACTION! GIANT ADVENTURE!

THE GUNSMITH

J.R. ROBERTS

penguin.com/actionwesterns

M455AS0509

LONGARM

GIANT-SIZED ADVENTURE FROM
AVENGING ANGEL LONGARM.

BY TABOR EVANS

2006 Giant Edition:

LONGARM AND THE
OUTLAW EMPRESS

2007 Giant Edition:

LONGARM AND THE
GOLDEN EAGLE SHOOT-OUT

2008 Giant Edition:

LONGARM AND THE
VALLEY OF SKULLS

2009 Giant Edition:

LONGARM AND THE
LONE STAR TRACKDOWN

penguin.com/actionwesterns

M456AS0409